Frozen
The Continuing Adventures of a Young Cowboy

Stu Campbell

ISBN: 978-0-9962019-2-6

6   5   4   3   2   1

Edited by Mira Perrizo
Cover and text design by D.K. Luraas
Cover painting by Larry Jones, Bouse, Arizona

Printed in the United States of America

Contents

Meeting New People

It was snowing when I left the ranch. I couldn't drive as fast as I wanted to because the roads were slick. I was anxious to see Sally and our new daughter and certainly didn't want to slide off the road. It was difficult to maintain a safe speed and still get to town. I felt like I was going to be late although I didn't have a time frame.

Bud had told me when I left, "Take your time, there's no rush."

I finally got to town and parked at the hospital parking lot. It was still snowing and I had to brush snow off my coat when I entered the hospital. I asked for Sally's room number at the information desk and found it. When I entered, Sally was sitting up in bed, resting.

"Hello, Daddy Honey!" Sally was in good spirits. "How does it feel to be a new father?"

"I don't know," I said. I gave Sally a kiss and she returned the favor. "I feel pretty much like I did before. Where's the baby?"

"She's in the nursery and she's beautiful! They'll be bringing her in before long for a feeding."

"How do you feel? How did it go?"

"I'm all right, and I'm glad it's over," said Sally. "The baby weighs seven pounds eight ounces and is twenty-one inches long. Missus Abercrombie was here earlier, she'll be back shortly. She's called your folks, they'll be here this afternoon. Your mother is very excited."

"What are we goin' to name it?" The baby was still an unknown element to me, not really a person yet. I hadn't even seen it yet.

"It is not an it," said Sally. "It is a child, a she or a her. Don't be calling her It!"

"Okay. What are we goin' to name her? Have you given it any thought?"

"I thought we could name her after my mother, or Missus Abercrombie," said Sally.

"She's too young to be called Missus Abercrombie," I said, teasing. "You've done a good job, we could name her after you, Sally Mae, an' call her Mae for short."

"No, silly! We could name her Virginia and call her Ginny for short. I never have liked the name Mae."

"Whatever you want," I said.

At that point, a nurse brought in our baby, wrapped in pink blankets. She handed the child to Sally for feeding.

I didn't get a good look at her. "Do you want me to leave?" I thought Sally might want some privacy while she was nursing the baby.

"No, you better get used to this," said Sally.

I sat down beside the bed and looked at the pamphlets that had been left by the nurses for new mothers. There was a lot of information there and I had to laugh at my thought, *We don't provide this information for our first calf heifers.*

Missus Abercrombie came back and gave me a disapproving look when she saw me. Sally noticed and said, "It's all right, I told him to stay. He has to get used to this."

"I got some things for you at the department store," said Missus Abercrombie, "the gift shop at the hospital is too expensive. Actually, they're for the baby."

Missus Abercrombie showed the items she'd bought to Sally. As she held them up, Sally's comments were, "That's cute," or "That's darling," or "Isn't that precious, Honey?"

I felt out of place and just nodded my head.

Soon, Sally was finished feeding the baby.

"Here, Dad, you hold her."

"I'm not sure just how to do this," I said, as I started to get up.

"You stay right where you are," said Missus Abercrombie. "I'll hand you the baby. This little darling can't be man-handled."

Missus Abercrombie took the baby from Sally and put her in my arms, explaining just how I should hold her. I had my first look at my daughter as I held her. For a minute, my daughter looked right into my eyes and I looked right at her. I wondered, what was she thinking? Then I wondered, can she think? I was beset with all kinds of questions about newborns that I couldn't answer.

"So, what do you think, Little Sis?"

"Talking to your daughter, Honey? That's good."

"Yeah," I answered, "but she ain't sayin' anythin.' I guess that's good, she ain't talkin' back. Maybe she don't like me."

Sally smiled. "She has to learn how to talk, silly. It'll take her a while."

I held the baby, sitting very motionless. I was about half scared. She was so small and appeared so fragile. I continued to talk to her, not really saying anything. It was a very one-sided conversation. I soon got tired of holding the baby and sitting so motionless.

"Here," I said, "I need to get up an' move around some."

Missus Abercrombie came over and took the baby from me. As we were exchanging the baby, my mother and father walked into the room.

My mother walked to me, said "Hello," gave me a kiss, and went straight to the baby. I was almost totally ignored.

My dad walked over, shook my hand and said, "Congratulations, son."

Missus Abercrombie gave the baby to my mother. "Isn't she darling? Sally has done a good job."

I was surprised at how adeptly my mother held the baby and gave Sally a hug and kiss at the same time. I wanted to shout out, "Be careful, don't drop her!" I decided not to, knowing that she'd had more experience handling newborns than I had.

My dad looked on without saying anything other than congratulating Sally. Sally, my mother, and Missus Abercrombie were busy discussing the baby. Dad and I were completely ignored.

"Come with me, son. Your mother has some things in the truck for the baby. We'll bring them in here."

Dad and I brought a couple of sacks from his truck to the hospital room. Sally looked surprised when she saw the gifts.

"Just a little something for my first grandchild," said my mother. "There's also a few things for you, Sally."

Sally, Missus Abercrombie, and my mother looked over the items in the sacks. It was just like Christmas. My dad and I looked on without saying anything.

Occasionally, Sally would ask, "Isn't this darling, Honey?"

I would just nod my head in agreement, not really thinking the item was "darling" but not wanting to argue the idea.

My dad and I started discussing the cow business.

Soon a nurse came and took the baby back to the nursery, saying, "It's time for her to get some sleep."

I didn't think that was necessary, since the baby was already sleeping.

"I don't know how we're going to get all this stuff home," said Sally. "Honey, can you take it back in your truck when you go? I'll figure out what I want to wear and what to dress the baby in and you can take the rest of it home with you."

"Yes, ma'am," I said. I knew I wasn't in charge of this situation.

"I'll help you carry the sacks to your truck," said Dad.

Sally picked out what she wanted for herself and the baby and Dad and I carried the remainder to my truck.

"Better put it all in the cab," said Dad. "You don't want it to get wet." It was still snowing. "I'm thinking it's about time we got something to eat. It's been a long time since breakfast. I'll buy you all something to eat if you want."

"I'll take you up on that," I said. "But I'm not really interested in hospital food."

"I'm in agreement with you on that," replied Dad.

When we arrived back at Sally's room, a nurse was herding my mother and Missus Abercrombie out of the room.

"This young lady needs some rest," said the nurse. "You can come back in a few hours."

Dad and I promptly told Mother and Missus Abercrombie that we were taking them to dinner. At dinner the conversation revolved around what we were going to name the baby. All kinds of suggestions were offered, but I remained silent.

"What's your ideas, Dad?" said my Dad.

"I'll let Sally make that decision," I said.

When we returned to Sally's room, she was resting, with the baby in a bassinette beside her. My folks made ready to leave, as Dad had chores to do back at the ranch. My mother found it difficult to leave the baby, being content to just hold her. However, she did leave with Dad, but only with a promise from Sally to keep her informed of the baby's progress.

A kiss from my mother, a handshake from my dad and a "thank you and drive careful" from Sally, and my folks left. It had stopped snowing.

"When do you have to go back?" asked Sally.

"Bud told me to take my time," I said. "I was thinkin' I'd spend the night an' go back tomorrow."

"Why don't you spend another day after that and follow us back to the ranch? I'd really feel better about it," said Sally.

"I could do that," I said. "I'll call Bud an' let him know. I'll get a room for tonight an' tomorrow night at the hotel."

I didn't really want to spend another day in town, but sometimes a feller has to do things he doesn't want to, just to keep peace in the family. I called the ranch and informed Bud of my decision.

"You just take all the time you want, my boy, there's nothing going on here that we can't handle," said Bud. After a few questions about Sally and the baby, we hung up.

The next day, I officially named the baby Virginia, with Sally's consent. Missus Abercrombie was very pleased.

"We'll call her Ginny," I said. "Then there won't be any confusion as to who I'm cussin' out."

Missus Abercrombie gave me a disapproving look, but quickly smiled. She was proud we named the child after her. I wasn't sure she appreciated my sense of humor.

I spent a lot of time visiting with Sally at the hospital and was relieved when we made preparation to leave the following day. Missus Abercrombie had brought the company car to the hospital entrance and a nurse wheeled Sally and Ginny to it. When they were all in the car, I told Missus Abercrombie, "You drive careful! That's my family you're chauffeurin' back to the ranch. I'll be right behind you."

We left for the ranch and the farther I got out of town, the better I felt. It had been somewhat stressful for me being in town without anything to do for three days.

Missus Abercrombie had taken me at my word and the trip back to the ranch was slow. *This is good,* I thought, although the road was still slick in some spots.

Our arrival at the ranch caused some commotion. Bud, Pat, Dwight, Chuck, and the cook were all waiting to meet the new addition to the Wilson Ranch. Congratulations were offered to Sally and me, although I didn't really know how to accept them. A simple thanks in reply didn't seem like enough and to say anything else seemed like too much.

The next few days were good. I had plenty to do and the monotony of town had left. We spent most of the morning handling the weaner colts. Then we rode through the cattle. It was a good time of year, cold at night and warming up nicely during the day.

Thanksgiving came and the cook outdid himself, as usual. I invited my folks up, but they declined.

"We've just seen the baby a few days ago. Perhaps we'll come at Christmas," was their reply.

Periodically, I would check in at the lodge, grab a cup of coffee and see how Sally and Ginny were doing. Ginny was generally sleeping, however Sally was losing a lot of sleep. Ginny had apparently gotten her days and nights mixed up and Sally was up at night quite a bit. Sally was kind enough not to wake me during the night, but I would often wake up. Missus Abercrombie was quick to admonish Sally and had her taking naps in the afternoon.

I had to take Sally and Ginny to town for Ginny's checkup and it was a nice break from the ranch. The doctor said Ginny was growing as she should, gaining weight but I couldn't see it.

"That's just because you're seeing her every day," said the doctor.

Christmas was getting close and I had Missus Abercrombie pick up some earrings for Sally and something for Ginny. What do you get a baby that's only about a month old? I had to get her something just so I wouldn't have a guilty conscience. I'd ordered some stuff for Pat, Dwight, and Chuck from a catalog. I left Bud's present for Sally to select.

I also had Missus Abercrombie pick up something for the cook. As far as I was concerned, Christmas was just a day to hurry through the chores and relax a little.

Sally had invited my folks for Christmas and they showed up a few days early, along with Tommy and Betty, my brother and sister. My mother immediately went for Ginny, showing surprise at how much she'd grown and how much she weighed. Tommy just showed a passing interest in Ginny, but Betty was completely enamored with her new niece.

"Who's doin' the chores at home?"

"There are no chores to do," answered my dad. "We won't have any real chores to do until after the first of the year, when we start feeding. So far it's been an open winter over at our place. It looks like it's been good here so far."

"One big snowstorm before Ginny was born has been the extent of our winter." I said. "We'll start feedin' the cows the first of January. Of course we've been feedin' the replacement heifers ever since we weaned them an' we have the first calvers in the feedlot. They'll get fed in the evenin'. There hasn't been much to do other than mess with the weaner colts an' the yearlings. How are the colts you bought from Bud comin' along? They should be pretty good horses by now."

"They're doing good," answered my dad. "Tommy has given your old horse, Charlie, to Betty. He's got a few years left in him yet. Tommy's been riding the one paint and I've been riding the other. We might have to get a few more horses shortly. Other than the two paints, all my horses are starting to show some age. Maybe we ought to look at your colts and start making some plans."

"We can do that in the mornin'," I said, "after we get the chores done. You can get a good look at 'em an' let me know what ones you're interested in."

"Tommy and I can help with the chores," said my dad.

"That won't be necessary," I said. "With Pat, Dwight, Chuck, an' myself, we got plenty of help. You just take it easy in the mornin'."

After the chores were done the next morning, my dad and I walked down to the barn. Pat, Dwight, and Chuck were already catching the weaner colts. Tommy was helping. We watched for a while then turned our attention to the coming two-year-olds.

"You're going to start riding these colts this winter," said my dad.

"Yep," I said. "They'll be old enough come January. At their age they won't stand a lot of ridin', just a little each day. I'm lookin' forward to it. Dwight and Chuck are lookin' forward to helpin' me. Dwight's already broke his first horse, a mustang filly we caught in with the broodmare bunch. He's been ridin' her, but she foaled awhile back an' has some time off. She appears to be comin' along good."

Dad looked over the coming two-year-olds and showed some interest in a couple of them. The colts had been halter broke the winter before and all were gentle. They came to the fence while we were talking and Dad and I were petting their noses and scratching their ears as we talked.

I asked him, "Do you want to buy one today?" I was just teasing.

"Not today," he said. "We'll see how their training comes along. There are some pretty wild-colored colts there. They should bring some pretty high prices."

"That's what we're hopin'," I said.

Dad and I rode through the cattle in the afternoon. This was mostly just a make-work project, the older cows generally did all right. We also rode through the weaner heifers and first calf heifers. Finding everything all right, we went back to the lodge to relax.

We found Betty holding Ginny, again.

"You're goin' to spoil my daughter," I said. "You might want to give her a break."

"That's what new nieces are for," replied Betty, "spoiling." She seemed perfectly content to watch the baby.

"You might have to give me a job this summer taking care of Ginny while Sally's out helping you with the dudes and cattle," she said.

"You ought to talk to Sally about that an' we'll take it under consideration. What would you charge us?"

"I'd do it for free," said Betty. "She's so cute. It would be fun."

"So you want to become a nanny?"

"That might be an idea," said Betty.

Christmas came and after the chores were done we spent the rest of the day visiting and exchanging gifts. Sally had gotten Tommy, Betty, and my parents something; I hadn't been to town to do any shopping. Even with the new baby, Sally managed to stay on top of everything.

I went to ride through the feedlot by myself, telling everyone, "You visit in here, I can handle this. I'll be back shortly." It was colder and I bundled up. Past experience had taught me that there's nothing as cold as horseback riding in the cold and I didn't like the cold.

When I returned, I was chilled to the bone and took a spot right in front of the fire.

A few days after Christmas, my folks left. It had got unseasonably cold and I spent a lot of time leading my horse on foot when I checked the feedlot just to keep my feet warm. We were lucky, we didn't have many sick cattle.

New Year's Eve came and it was pretty mellow. Pat didn't fire his shotgun in the air as was his custom; he didn't want to wake up Ginny. The following day we would feed the cows in the afternoon. The first calvers would also be fed in the afternoon. This practice would encourage the cattle to calve in the mornings rather than at odd hours during the night.

Losing an Old Friend

We'd turned the saddle horses out, except for the horses we were going to use during the winter. I kept Roman and Drygulch in for me. I also kept in Sally's big paint that Bud had given her and her grulla horse, Beauty. Pat kept his private horse and one other, Dwight kept his mustang mare and one paint, and Chuck kept in the other paint and one dude horse. When we started riding the two-year-olds, we could give our regular saddle horses a rest.

I made Dwight tie up his mustang's colt when he used the mare. I didn't think we needed a colt running loose and getting in the way while we were doing our work. I convinced him that we should put the colt with the other weaner colts and we could start working with her when we were working the other colts.

"That will give the colt some company. Horses are pretty gregarious an' they need company," I said.

He thought this was a good idea and it made sense. He put the colt with the other weaner colts.

Occasionally, we'd ride through the saddle horses just to check on them and even more infrequently, we'd check the broodmare bunch. Quite often we could check on the broodmares from the truck. That made it easy, the truck had a heater.

Dwight, Chuck, and I would load the hay in the mornings for the afternoon feeding. Occasionally during these times, Pat would ride through the saddle horses.

We started breaking the two-year-olds in January. Pat's horses made good snubbing horses and the four horses I kept in also made good snubbing horses. Dwight and Chuck could do the riding for the colt's first few rides.

About the middle of January, Pat checked the saddle horses. He came back with some disturbing news. "I didn't see your donkey, Matilda, out there," he said. "I thought I'd go out again tomorrow an' look for her. Do you want to go?"

"I'd probably better," I said. "Sally will be really concerned if somethin's happened to her. You know I gave Matilda to her awhile back, after Einstein was foaled."

The next day, Pat and I saddled up. It had started to snow, but it wasn't as cold as it had been earlier in the week. When we got to the pasture where the saddle horses were, Pat and I split up. We could cover more ground separately than together. I got a chance to look over the saddle horses and they were wintering well. If there had been any problems with any of them, Pat would have let me know or brought the horse in for some treatment.

Soon I saw Pat coming toward me at an extended trot. *He must have found somethin'*, I thought. I started riding to meet him.

"I found Matilda," said Pat. "She won't be comin' back to the ranch. It looks like she just laid down, went to sleep an' died. Einstein ain't too far away."

"Damn," I said. I wasn't in the habit of cussing and it just slipped out. Although she was old, this came as a shock. "Where is she?"

"Over this way about three quarters of a mile."

We started toward Matilda. When we got to her, it was just like Pat had said. I marked the spot and we headed back to the ranch. It was a sober ride back and I reflected on the times Matilda and I had spent together. I had traded some of my wages for her and used her as a pack animal to ride home.

We must have made a funny sight, riding along the highway. Then Matilda had Sassy and that even added to the sight. I often thought we must have looked like misplaced gypsies. A lot of people took our pictures along the way.

Later on that summer, Bud's brother, Rod, had saved her and Sassy from an attack from a mountain lion.

Then there was the time she, Roman, and Sassy got stolen from the rodeo grounds when I'd got hurt in the bareback bronc riding. The sheriff of that county had radioed that my animals were missing and a highway patrolman had pulled the culprits over on a drunk driving charge. It was George Crawford that had stolen them and Pat and I had caught him trying to steal one of our colts. I smiled as I thought, *He's still in the pen.*

Matilda had been bred by Bud's paint stud due to an oversight on everyone's part, hence Einstein came into being. I gave Matilda to Sally along with Einstein. Matilda had brought a lot of happy times to the youngsters that were too little to ride. She had contributed a lot to the ranch and had more than paid her way.

After supper that night, I announced, "Matilda has passed away. I'm goin' to take the Skidster an' bury her tomorrow."

"Oh no," said Sally. "Ginny hasn't even had a chance to know her." Sally was visibly shaken. She had spent a lot of time with Matilda and the younger children.

Bud wheeled his chair over and put his arm around Sally in an effort to console her. "It's all right, Daughter. Things like this happen. Death is as much a part of life as birth."

Sally was saddened by the news, and I didn't know what to say other than, "Einstein is here, he can do her job."

The next day, I took the Skidster to where Matilda was and started to dig a grave. It was hard digging, the ground was frozen and I had to dig a big hole in order to drive the Skidster out. It took longer than I expected but I finally got the job done. Unceremoniously, I pushed Matilda into the hole.

"Goodbye old girl. It's been good." I found myself talking out loud to myself as I buried her. "I'll bring a marker out in the spring." I put a big rock over the grave to mark it with the Skidster. It was probably about four foot around.

The trip back to the ranch was slow in the Skidster as I reflected more about Matilda. I had originally named her Sally, but changed her name to Matilda after meeting Sally Wilson. I didn't want to embarrass Sally or me.

By the time I got back to the ranch, it was dinnertime. After dinner, it was time to start the evening chores.

The first of February was approaching and the first calf heifers should start calving. I started looking for the springing heifers as I rode through them. Quite often, I had Dwight or Chuck riding with me, sometimes both of them. Chuck had done some calving out before, but it was all new to Dwight. I had to show him what to look for and explain what was going to happen and the various problems we could expect. Dwight looked forward to calving. To me it was just another necessary chore.

They would have to watch the heifers when I took Sally and Ginny to town for Ginny's checkups. I would be able to leave feeling confidant that things would be all right. Pat would also be around to give them a hand if they needed it.

Although I didn't really like going to town, especially during the winter, it did give me a chance to get out of the winter weather. We hadn't had much snow, and the lack of cloud cover at night allowed what heat that had accumulated during the day to escape. Consequently, it was cold. I found myself wishing for a good snowstorm, perhaps to help raise the daytime temperature and we needed the moisture.

The first week in February, it began to snow and we got about a foot and a half in one day. We had some calves on the ground and I really liked having the shed to afford the calves some protection. It was still snowing the next day, although not as hard.

Bud was bundled up and out in the Skidster early, plowing snow. I think he really enjoyed driving the Skidster and having a job to do with it gave him a sense of purpose.

Occasionally, Sally would come to the barn, saddle a horse and ride through the heifers with me. The first time she showed up, my first question was, "Who's watchin' Ginny?"

"Missus Abercrombie is doing a good job," replied Sally. "And Daddy's there also."

Sally enjoyed riding with me and she was getting back into shape. Every now and then, she'd take her lariat rope down and heel a calf, without dallying up, just for practice. She was a good roper. She'd also show up at the corrals when we were breaking the colts just to help out. With the baby and trying to help out with the horse breaking and checking the heifers she stayed pretty busy. When she was in the lodge, she also took care of the reservations.

On one trip to town for Ginny's checkup, Sally said, "Our reservations are full from the middle of May until about the middle of July. Into August and September, we only have a limited amount of space available for dudes. We even have some reservations for early October. It looks like we'll have a better year than last year. I'm looking forward to it. We might take in a few dudes earlier in May if we have the requests and the weather holds."

"That's good," I said. "But don't you ever get tired of all the people around?"

"Sometimes it does get to me, but the trick is not to let the guests know it," said Sally. "The secret is providing each guest the best experience possible and making them feel like they are genuinely important."

"You an' Bud are good at that," I said. "But sometimes it's quite a chore for me to pretend that much."

Sally laughed. "You're getting better at it."

On our return to the ranch, Dwight approached me. "I had

a phone call today," he said. "My dad is sick and not expected to live much longer. I need to go home for a while."

"Certainly. You need to take care of your family matters," I said. I hadn't given much thought to the hired help's family, although occasionally I noticed a letter or package come for them. "How long will you be gone?"

"I don't know," said Dwight. "It's a pretty serious situation. But I will be back, I just don't know when. I don't want you to think of me like that other guy that you hired and were counting on, and then he left."

"No," I said. "You do what you have to do. Just keep in touch an' let us know what's happenin'. I'll have Sally make a check out for you, you can cash it when you go through town so you'll have some travelin' money. When are you leavin'?"

"I'll go first thing in the morning. It's a little late to go now."

"That's good," I said. "You can get breakfast, then travel. Take all the time you need."

I told Sally and Bud what was happening and asked Sally to make out a check for Dwight. "Depending on how long he's gone," I said, "you might have to have Missus Abercrombie take you to town for Ginny's checkup. I don't know if I'll be able to get away."

The next morning Dwight left right after breakfast. Chuck asked, "Do you think he'll be back?"

"He'll be back," I said. "He hasn't packed up all his stuff an' his mustang an' her colt are still here. He thinks quite a bit of that mustang. He'll be back."

"While he's gone, I'll get to ride more of them colts," said Chuck.

"Maybe I'll have a chance to ride some of 'em," I said. "You can't have all the fun! But his bein' gone will mean a little more work for all of us. We still have the colts to ride, heifers to check, cows to feed an' the cows will start calvin' soon. We'll have plenty to do. And don't forget, we can still mess with the weaner colts. The more we handle 'em, the better they'll get."

"But we can start using the colts to check the cattle," said Chuck. "That should help out a bunch."

"Yes," I said. "But we'll have to be changin' horses frequently. Those colts can't take a lot of ridin'. An' there's a lot of mud in the feedlot. That's pretty hard work on a young horse, any horse for that matter."

"I'll bet we can handle it!"

We got busier during Dwight's absence and I hadn't realized how much an extra man lightened the day's chores. However, it was better to be busy than have a lot of idle time.

Later on in February, we got more snow. And it continued to snow, adding to the difficulties. The snow got deep enough that Bud was out every day in the Skidster clearing it away. It was really helpful in getting the gates in the feedlot to swing open easily, without getting off a horse to open them.

Dwight called once a week. His father's situation hadn't changed and Dwight was concerned we wouldn't hold his job for him. Bud answered his call one time and told him, "Don't worry. You've got a job as long as we can count on you. Just keep in touch."

We had most of the heifers calved out, and had lost two calves, when the cows started to calve in the first part of March. We managed to get a couple of day-old calves from the dairy and grafted them onto the heifers. Pat pretty well took care of the cows while Chuck and I watched the heifers. We all fed the cows together.

Occasionally, Pat would bring a cow to the calving sheds and have to pull a calf. Chuck and I would help. We'd keep the cow and calf in a pen for a few days then take her and the calf back to the main cow herd.

We didn't want to, but we started feeding the saddle horses. Once we started, we'd have to keep it up, the horses wouldn't get out and rustle up feed, they'd wait by the gate for the feed to be brought to them. It meant extra chores but it was necessary. Even though the days were getting longer, it was taking longer to do the chores. We even ran the broodmare bunch closer to the ranch and started feeding them.

Dwight called. His father had passed away and he told us he'd be back in a week or ten days. Sally had taken the call and told him, "You take care of things there and show up when you can."

It continued to snow in March. I was glad to see it, as it meant more water and that meant more grass, even if it was inconvenient now.

When Dwight showed up, he was driving a newer pickup. "It was my dad's," he said. "It's about all he had. I guess I'll drive it about as long as I can." Dwight didn't seem to be affected by his father's death, and went right to work. He'd had a week or ten days to get used to his father's passing and seemed to adjust to it well.

I wondered what his relationship with his father was and questioned him about it.

"My dad had been sick for quite a while and his health was declining steadily. His death didn't come as a big surprise, we had been expecting it and prepared for it for quite a while."

I asked, "Why didn't you stick around longer while he was still alive?"

Dwight smiled. "My dad told me, 'There's no need for you to hang around waiting for me to die. I can do that,' he said. 'You go out and start your own life.' With his permission, I left. There wasn't much I could do there. My mother and sisters pretty well took care of him. I did see him for a few days before he died."

"Sounds like he had a lot of guts," I said.

"Yep. He knew what was happening and simply faced it."

Dwight's arrival lightened the workload on everyone, especially when we were loading hay. We all expressed our condolences about his father's passing and went right back to work.

Spring

The first day of spring arrived and with it came more snow, another foot. It was a heavy, wet snow with a lot of water content. And it continued to snow. Bud was out every day, pushing snow out of the way.

"That'll melt before too long," I said.

"Perhaps," said Bud. "But when it gets moved around a little, it melts faster. I'll get in these pens this summer after you've moved the cattle out and fix it so it drains a little easier. All this moisture has created a drainage problem for us. I want to get this done so I can interview at the college for summer help next month. We'll be a little late doing that this year, but it has to be done."

"Are you goin' to take Sally with you?"

"Yes," replied Bud, "and Ginny, too, if she wants to go."

"She'll want to go, all right," I said. "All we need are some maids an' a cook's helper. Dwight an' Chuck have already told me that they want to stay for the summer."

"That's good," said Bud. "We'll probably leave during the middle of April. I'll make room arrangements."

Dwight and I went to the bull pasture, sorted out the Black Angus bull and brought him to the feedlot. He'd be ready to catch the heifers we didn't get bred artificially. We put him in a separate pen.

"Ain't it kinda early to be bringing him here?"

"It is a little early," I said. "But Sally tells me we're full up with dudes in the last part of May an' into June an' July. We're doin' this now so we don't have to do it later an' we can spend more time with the dudes. We'll be ready. I sorta like to stay on top of things."

We were about done calving out the first calf heifers and turned our attention to the main cow herd. Dwight, Chuck, and I were riding the two-year-old colts on a regular basis. Sally was coming down to the barn, saddling a horse and coming out with us on a regular basis. Missus Abercrombie was doing a good job of looking after Ginny and Bud was even helping out, giving the baby rides on his motorized wheelchair frequently, when it was warm enough. Ginny seemed to enjoy it, and if she was fussing, it seemed to calm her.

I noticed a few straight black and black bally calves being born among the first calf heifers and thought they might have been the result of the Black Angus bull we'd turned in as a clean up bull. I'd be better able to tell as they grew. I hoped we had enough calves to justify purchasing the bull—I'd paid more than I wanted to for him. I made a mental note to sort off the Angus cross calves from the Longhorn crosses when we weaned.

April arrived and it was still snowing an inch or two every night it seemed. We were done calving the first calvers and started moving cows and calves to the proper pastures. The main cow herd was calving on a regular basis; a few new calves were showing up every morning. We did come across a dead calf one morning and it didn't take long to find the tight-bagged cow. Pat and I roped her and Chuck marked her with a grease stick.

"We might want to make hamburger out of her for the summer guests," said Pat. "We'll need plenty anyway. We'll put her in the feedlot before we turn out the cows on the Forest Service land for the summer."

About the middle of April, when Bud, Sally, and Ginny returned from the college interviewing sessions, I asked Bud, "What if Sally an' I were to take a couple or three days at the end of the month an' take a little vacation? Our second anniversary's comin', and we're goin' to be busy with the dudes. That's the only time we could go. I don't know what else to do; I'd like to do somethin'. You know, I entirely forgot our first anniversary."

"That's a great idea, Honey. Why don't you do it? Where would you go?"

"I don't know," I said. "I haven't really given it much thought. Right now it's just an idea."

"Why don't you go spend a few days with your folks? I know they'd like to see Ginny and you could relax some there."

"I'll call 'em an' see if it's all right," I said. "Don't say anything to Sally; I'd sorta like this to be a surprise."

"Good enough," said Bud. "Just let me know."

I called my folks that night and they said they'd be delighted to have us spend a couple of days. My mother reminded me, "You make sure you bring Ginny. I'll take care of her and Sally can get some rest."

I made arrangements to show up around the first of May, give or take a day or two.

The next day, I was riding through the cow herd with Pat. We noticed a cow that wasn't just right and we roped her and gave her a shot of penicillin. I didn't know just what was wrong, but something wasn't quite right.

"We'll look for her tonight when we feed an' see how she's doin'," said Pat.

"That's all we can do," I said.

I was a little surprised. It was past the middle of April, there was still snow on the ground and we were still feeding. I hoped our feed held out.

When we fed that night, we looked for our sick cow. We

found her and she seemed to be improving so we left her. We had put cows in separate pastures and we had about fifty cows in each pasture. Feeding involved opening and closing gates between each pasture. It was a necessary nuisance, but it worked into our pasture rotation system.

The next day, Pat and I went out to look for the sick cow and we found her. She appeared to be all right.

"I wonder what was wrong with her," I said.

"I don't know," said Pat. "Maybe she had somethin' like the twenty-four hour flu like we get. I think she'll be all right. We'll just look for her every day."

I told Pat of my plans to visit my folks for a few days. "That's a good idea," he said. "I think your daughter needs to get to know her other grandpa. Bud has been spending a lot of time with her. He might even be spoilin' her some."

"You're right!" And I laughed at the mental picture I formed of Bud wheeling her around in his wheelchair. "While we're gone, you might want to run in the saddle horses an' start ridin' 'em. We don't want any surprises. We'll have to run in the broodmares an' brand the colts when I get back."

"I figured we'd get around to that pretty soon," said Pat.

On the twenty-eighth of April, I told Sally, "Pack some things for you an' Ginny, we're goin' to be gone for a few days."

Sally looked surprised. "What?"

"That's right Darlin,' we're takin' a few days vacation. Get packed or I'm goin' without you."

"What's this all about?"

"We have an anniversary comin' up," I said. "Accordin' to you, we're goin' to be very busy on our anniversary day, so I thought we'd take off for a few days early. You know, I forgot our first anniversary last year, we got so busy, so I thought I'd better do somethin' this year. This is your anniversary present."

"Where are we going?"

"I thought we'd go spend a few days at my folks," I said. "I think it's time we introduced Ginny to her other grandma an' grandpa. She might even remember 'em now."

"That's a wonderful idea," said Sally. "I'll be ready in ten minutes."

Soon we were headed out. We took my truck as Bud needed the car. It was a long day's drive to my folks place and we stopped in town to get something to eat.

As we were eating, I noticed the clouds building up. "It might not have been such a bad idea to take the truck," I said. "It looks like it's goin' to storm. Here it is the end of April an' we're still gettin' snow! Havin' the truck with four-wheel drive is a good idea. Besides that, you've packed enough, we couldn't get it all in the car."

Sally just laughed and tended to Ginny. When we left town it was snowing. By the time we got to my folks' place, there was an inch of snow on the ground.

We unloaded Sally's and Ginny's stuff with the help of Tommy, my brother. We got done just in time to help Dad feed. He was feeding in the afternoon just as we were.

Ginny made a big hit with both my mother and Betty, my sister. I just watched passively as they fussed over Ginny and Ginny was responding to them. They thoroughly enjoyed the youngster.

The next day, I went out with Dad to check the cows. There were six inches of new snow on the ground when we left. Betty had volunteered her horse, Charlie, for me to ride. Charlie had been my horse, but I had given him to Tommy one year for Christmas. Tommy, in turn, had given him to Betty when Dad had bought a couple of spotted colts from Bud. It was kinda nice to ride Charlie again, I hadn't ridden him for a few years and although he was getting old, he still had plenty of energy. It almost seemed like he liked being ridden.

Dad and I discussed the cow business as we rode and looked

over his cattle. He was about calved out and had a good calving percentage so far. Then he changed the subject.

"You know," said Dad, "your sister has been buggin' me about comin' to your place this summer and takin' care of Ginny. How do you feel about it?"

"She'd have to talk to Sally about that," I said. "I know Sally's countin' a lot on Missus Abercrombie to help out this summer, but she's gettin' a little old. I don't know if she can do very much. Betty might be some good help, but how do you an' Mom feel about it?"

"Your mother thinks it's a good idea, but she would certainly miss Betty all summer," replied Dad.

"Betty needs to talk to Sally about that," I said. "Betty might be some good help; Sally says we're full all the way into August now. Sally's in charge of Ginny. I just get to look at her an' hold her every now an' then. Whatever they decide is okay with me. Would you bring her over?"

My dad laughed. "We could bring her over after school lets out."

"Would you pick her up in the fall?"

My dad laughed again. "Yes."

I noticed Betty was spending a lot of time with Sally and Ginny during our visit and I thought perhaps my sister was bribing my wife about a summer job.

We spent three days relaxing at my folks. I did help Dad pull one calf, but didn't do much else. My time was spent mostly just loafing and I was becoming a little restless. Betty spent a little time around me, questioning me about her summer employment as a nanny.

"I don't know about that," I said. "I'm only in charge of the wranglers. I don't have much to do with the domestic help. You'll have to talk to Sally about that."

"You are just like Mom and Dad," said Betty.

"What do you mean?"

"I ask Mom a question," said Betty, "and she says, 'go ask your father.' Then I ask Dad and he says, 'go ask your mother.' It's very frustrating! Back and forth, back and forth, just like a Ping Pong ball! When I asked Sally about it, she said 'go ask your brother,' and you say 'go ask Sally.' I haven't got an answer from anyone yet."

I laughed. "I'll ask Sally about it for you. How does Mother feel about it?"

"I don't know," said Betty. "She just says 'go ask your father.' Back and forth, back and forth!"

After supper that night, I asked Sally, "How do you feel about Betty comin' out this summer an' helpin' keep an eye on Ginny?"

"I think it's a good idea," said Sally. "Missus Abercrombie could supervise Betty and be around if she needed some help. Betty's what, twelve now? She's old enough. And Missus Abercrombie is getting a little older. Ginny might be too much for her to handle when she starts walking. She could also help out watching the guests' kids. I told Betty to ask you."

"I know," I said. "Betty told me we were just like Mom an' Dad, 'go ask Sally, go ask Honey.' She feels like a Ping Pong ball, back an' forth, back an' forth. At supper, I'll tell her she can come, but I'll have a little fun with her first. In the meantime, you just send her to me an' I'll keep sendin' her back to you. If she wants this job, we'll make her work for it!"

"You're mean," said Sally, grinning.

"Perhaps, but we'll have some fun."

That night at supper, Betty asked both Sally and me, "Are you going to make a decision about me working for you this summer? Or, have you made a decision?"

"We have arrived at a decision," I said, "but only after a goodly amount of consideration. It was very difficult to reach a conclusion. How badly do you want to come this summer?"

"Very badly," said Betty.

"How much would you be willin' to pay us to come to work for us?"

My mother showed some surprise at this comment, but I saw my dad grinning slightly.

"I don't have much money," said Betty. "How much would you charge me?" The question had caught Betty by surprise and I took advantage of the situation.

"I think you'd have to pay us somethin'," I said. "We'd have to give Missus Abercrombie some money to watch both you an' Ginny. An' it would cost us to feed you. You know, we're a dude ranch an' we charge people to come an' stay with us! That's how we make our livin'."

Sally was having a hard time controlling her laughter. She finally had to get up and make a pretense of caring for Ginny.

"I'm not a dude," said Betty. "Besides that, if I'm working taking care of Ginny, you're supposed to pay me! And Missus Abercrombie doesn't have to watch me. I'm twelve years old!"

Showing surprise, I said, "Is that how it works?"

"Yes." Betty felt proud that she had made her point.

"How much would you eat? Maybe we could feed you what the dudes didn't eat."

"I don't eat much," said Betty. "And I would be a big help."

I relented. "We have decided to let you come if it's okay with Mom. You talk to Sally about what she'll pay you."

Betty was excited and jumped up and gave me a big hug. "Can I bring Sassy?"

"No," I said. "We have Einstein. He can do the job."

"What happened to Matilda?"

"Matilda was old," I said. "She just laid down one night

an' died." It occurred to me that I hadn't told the family about Matilda.

Betty was disturbed by the news. But it didn't take long for her to get over it now that she knew she could come for the summer. "I'll get packed right away," she said. "I can go back with you tomorrow!"

"Wait a minute, young lady," said my mother. "You still have a month of school to go."

My sister's reply was a meek, "Oh yeah, I forgot."

I told Betty what she'd need to pack. "Dad will bring you out after school's out."

We left the next morning to go back to the Wilson Ranch. The snow that had fallen was a heavy, wet snow and it had pretty well melted when we left. The roads back to the ranch were dry.

"We have guests coming in two weeks," said Sally. "Are you ready?"

"As ready as I'll ever be," I said. "I hope Pat an' the boys started ridin' the saddle horses. That's one job that we won't have to mess with."

Breaking in a New Hand

Bud greeted us when we got to the ranch. Dwight and Chuck helped me unload the truck.

"How are your folks? Did they winter well?" Bud was always careful to inquire into the well being of everyone.

"They're fine," I said. "They send their best to you. Are things here all right?"

"Oh yes," said Bud. "We even have some guests here now. Sally isn't the only one that can make money for this outfit! And I've got a few reservations for September. They're on the board."

Bud was quite proud of his achievement, but that is what this business is all about.

Sally overheard Bud's comment. "How many people do we have?"

"Just a couple," said Bud. "By the way, Jim, our head housekeeper called. His job at the ski area is permanent, but only during the winter, from November to April. I hired him and told him he could count on a permanent summer job here. He'll be here in two or three days."

"That's good," said Sally. "The three girls we hired at the college will be here toward the end of May. Jim and I can handle things until then. And I hired a nanny for Ginny for the summer."

"A nanny? I sorta thought I'd do that job," said Bud.

"We hired Honey's sister," said Sally. "You can help her when I'm not around."

"Well, that's all right," said Bud. "Keep it in the family. Before you know it, we'll have a going concern here."

Chuck said, "We've been riding the saddle horses. There's nothing out of the ordinary happening there."

"That's good," I said. "I think we're right on schedule. Do our guests want to ride tomorrow?"

"I don't know," said Chuck. "They're out on a ride with Pat and Dwight now."

"If they had a good time, they'll probably want to go tomorrow. We'll take 'em someplace where they ain't been. We'll have to figure out who's goin' to take 'em, the rest of us will bring in the broodmares an' brand the colts."

"I'd sure like to bring in the broodmares," said Chuck. "That can be some pretty wild riding."

"It can be a lot of fun," I said. "But it's kinda slick out there. It might be a little dangerous."

"That just adds to the fun," said Chuck. "Ain't there a certain element of danger involved every time we get horseback?"

"True," I said. "But it might be a little more dangerous bringin' in the broodmares."

When Pat and Dwight got back, I recognized their riders. They had stayed with us last year—they were the first guests we had. But, I couldn't remember their names. However, I greeted them like I knew them and I put up a pretty good front for a while, and then finally said, "You know, I'm too honest to continue this. I'm embarrassed, but I can't remember your names."

"Pat told us you'd probably try to buffalo us. We just thought we'd let you go on and see how long it took you to fess up. We're Dan and Polly Stanford. We were here last year, early."

"That's right," I said. I smiled, "Of course that's right. You ought to remember your own names. I just can't remember 'em. But, I remember now. We've had a lot of people here an' it's difficult to remember everyone. Sally will be anxious to see you an' show off our new addition. She's up at the lodge. We'll take care of your horses, you can go up an' visit with her."

Pat came up to me, grinning. "Its kinda hard to remember everyone, ain't it?"

"Yeah," I said. "Especially when I don't have the benefit of Sally's board. What do you have in mind for tomorrow? Do they want to ride again?"

"They're leavin' in the mornin'. What do you have planned?"

"I thought we'd run in the broodmares an' brand the colts," I said. "We need to do that before we get too many guests in."

"Tomorrow would be a good day," agreed Pat.

The next day we saddled up to gather the broodmares. I had Chuck and Dwight saddle their older, well broke horses. "Sometimes these colts get a little excited when we're runnin' in the horses an' cause some problems." I saddled my horse, Roman.

Sally came down and saddled her grulla. "I've missed this fun for a while," she said. "I'm going to help you today."

I asked, "Is Ginny goin' to be all right?"

"Yes," answered Sally. "Daddy and Missus Abercrombie are watching her. She'll be fine."

Pat had replaced his lariat rope with his bull whip. "You never know," he said, when he saw me watching him.

When we found the mares, I said, "Sally an' I will lead 'em in if you guys want to follow. Just don't run 'em over us!"

Pat grinned. "We'll try not to."

Sally and I hit a brisk trot in front of the mares and it wasn't long before we had them corralled. Bud and Missus Abercrombie were in the four-wheeler outside the corral. Bud was holding Ginny and Missus Abercrombie had a disgusted look on her face.

Pat caught the stud and tied him outside the corral. I took

32

Sally's horse and tied him outside the corral as Sally went to Ginny.

"What do you think of this, little girl? This is the first time you've seen the horses run in," said Sally.

"It's disgusting to bring an infant into this dusty, dirty environment," said Missus Abercrombie.

"The dust will wash off, Virginia," said Bud. "She's starting her education early, just like her mom did. Besides that, there isn't that much dust."

Sally had picked up Ginny. "Did you miss me?" Sally was brushing off the dust from Ginny's face.

Ginny was focusing all her attention on the horses stirring around in the corral. It was quite a sight and quite colorful.

"I brought the camera," said Bud, "but didn't get the fire started."

"That's all right," I said. "Dwight has started the fire. Are you ready to take pictures, Darlin'?"

Sally handed Ginny to Bud. "As soon as the irons are hot," she said.

I roped the first colt. Dwight and Chuck braced him against the fence and Pat branded him. Sally took his picture for registration purposes.

We branded all morning and Ginny and Bud sat outside the corral watching. Missus Abercrombie stayed around the corral, no doubt looking for an opportunity to remove her namesake from the dusty, dirty environment.

When we were done, Sally brought her horse over, got on and said, "Hand me Ginny, Honey. Then get your horse. We'll have someone take our picture. We might make Christmas cards for the future. Pat, get the camera, please."

Everyone did as ordered and Sally made sure we had plenty of pictures from all different angles. When she was satisfied, she handed me Ginny.

"Give her back to her grandpa. We can take these horses back now."

We took the horses back to their range and turned them loose. Coming through the saddle horse pasture, I showed Sally where I'd buried Matilda.

On the ride home, Sally said, "I'm surprised Ginny didn't fall asleep while we were branding. I'll bet she sleeps good tonight!"

"There was a lot goin' on," I said. "She'd never seen it before. Just like Bud said, she's startin' her education early. I wonder how much of it she'll remember."

"She'll remember it all," said Sally.

"Because of the pictures?"

"I also took a lot of pictures of her and Daddy. She'll remember it when we show her those! And I got some of Missus Abercrombie trying to keep her face clean. Missus Abercrombie won't think those pictures are very flattering. She has her disgusted look on her face."

"If you say so," I said. I wasn't sure. "Was Missus Abercrombie tryin' to keep her face clean or Ginny's?" I thought Missus Abercrombie's disgusted look was her normal look. I decided not to mention this thought to Sally.

Sally laughed. "I suppose she was trying to keep both their faces clean."

The next day, Jim, who had been our head housekeeper the last few years, showed up. We also had some more people drop in. Sally explained to them that while we had plenty of room now, in two more days we would be full and couldn't accommodate them after that.

They agreed and had a good time while they were there. They did a lot of riding and were very happy—happy enough to make reservations for the following year. That made Sally very happy.

"We've got some entries on our board for next year already," she said, after the people left. "That's what I call starting out right."

"Keep up the good work, Daughter," said Bud. "That's what makes this place operate!"

"I suppose," I said, "that the tourist season has started. There's no turnin' back now." I geared myself up for a tough season. We looked to be busy the whole summer.

We had the horseshoer come and he spent a few days putting shoes on all the saddle horses. He brought a helper and Chuck gave him a hand. It didn't take long to get all the horses shod. I had him put shoes on Einstein. With Betty coming to help out with Ginny and the other kids, I thought the hinny might get a lot of use during the summer.

We'd finished calving and had put the little cow herds in their different pastures. Now about all we had to do was take care of the dudes, move some cattle around, and brand a few calves every couple of weeks. On the surface, it looked like a fairly easy summer, but I knew the guests could make it very difficult or very easy. I also knew it could be a combination of both.

The next day, Bud went to town. When he returned he had two car seats and an extra diaper bag. "Put one of those in the four-wheeler and put it in good. There's no reason why Ginny can't go with me when I go out to look things over. Daughter," he said, handing the diaper bag to Sally, "put some extra diapers and such in here. If she's going to go with her grandpa, she's going to go in style!"

Sally smiled and did as she was told. She was glad that her dad was going to bring Ginny to whatever ranch functions he could get to with the four-wheeler. Sally could participate in the ranch functions horseback and still keep an eye on her baby. I quietly approved.

We got a few drop-ins and those people would stay for a day or two. Sally was pleased, it meant some extra money. If Sally couldn't get a reservation from the people, she made sure they left with our literature.

"You just never know," she said. "Some of them might come back. I think I'll make up some new pamphlets. I'll use one of the pictures Pat took when we branded the colts and stress the family aspect. I think we'll go full color. I could enclose one with each of our newsletters."

I was surprised Sally was still sending out newsletters. I'd been busy enough I hadn't even read one for a couple of months.

"Maybe you an' Bud ought to discuss raisin' the prices a little an' print 'em on pamphlets for next year," I said. "Everything else is goin' up an' maybe we need to keep up with the times."

"You'll need to discuss it with us," said Sally. "You're just as much a part of this as we are."

The first part of May, we started artificially breeding the yearling heifers. We'd have to ride through the heifers morning and night to pull out the ones that were exhibiting heat, or the "bullers" as we called them.

The guests started arriving on a regular basis beginning the middle of May and Sally and I tried to be there when they arrived to greet them. I recognized a lot of them, but had a hard time remembering their names. Sally made it easier on me. When she would introduce them to me, she would say, "This is the Smith family, John and Joyce. You remember them from last year, don't you?"

"Of course," I would say, then stick out my hand and say, "How are you doin'?" or "It looks like you wintered well." I thought we pulled it off pretty good, but I'm sure Sally would fess up at a later date, much to the amusement of the guests.

As we selected horses for the guests, I could remember them easier by the horses they'd ridden in the past. I thought that was strange.

The first weekend after we were officially opened, we were completely full. It was tough on Sally, Missus Abercrombie, and Jim, cleaning rooms, making beds and the like. Our maid help hadn't shown up; they weren't due for another week or ten days. I felt sorry for Sally, trying to clean rooms and take care of Ginny at the same time. Missus Abercrombie was showing the wear and tear also. I volunteered to help, but my services were declined.

"We can do a better job without you!"

I was relieved I didn't have to help clean the rooms. I didn't know anything about it and was just trying to be helpful.

Quite often Bud would take Ginny either in the motorized wheelchair or in the four-wheeler. He didn't do it every day, he'd gotten busy cleaning the corrals with the Skidster. This helped Sally out and on those days when Bud did babysit, she wasn't nearly as tired as when he didn't.

Pat, Dwight, Chuck, and I stayed busy taking the guests out on horseback rides. I pretty much rode the heifer pens pulling the "bullers" early in the morning and later on in the afternoon. The inseminator had arrived and we would breed the heifers in the afternoon. One of us had to help the inseminator and we'd take turns.

We took the guests out on mostly scenic, walking rides. We had a lot of fun, joking with the guests and the scenery was great. The grass was coming and everything was green. I didn't want to brand any calves until Betty arrived and could help with Ginny.

The maids arrived a few days early and I was glad to see them. With three girls to do the domestic chores, that job became easier. The girls didn't get the benefit of any formal training. They went right to work—it was on-the-job training. Missus Abercrombie was forced by Sally to take a break, and although she protested, she did relax. She would have worked until she dropped. I began to have a new admiration for the woman.

I couldn't convince Sally to take a break. "I'll have to help out for a few more days until we get the new girls trained, then I'll take it easy," she'd say. I could tell she was getting tired.

My mom and dad brought Betty one morning. It was nice to see Betty, I knew Sally's job would become easier. My mother went straight to Ginny while Betty and I took her stuff to the room where she would be staying.

"You must have left real early this mornin'," I said to my dad.

"Actually," said Dad, "we left yesterday afternoon and stayed in the hotel in town. Sally has been talking with your mother and she indicated you were full as far as accommodations go. We thought it would be easier on everyone."

"That was good thinking," I said. "I don't know where we'd have put you up."

"Does Betty have everything? We need to be heading back," said Dad. "Where is she?"

Betty and my mother were fussing over Ginny. Mother was reluctant to leave. A hug and a kiss to Sally and Ginny and Mother said, "We have a long way to go. Betty you make sure Sally calls once a week and you do a good job!"

"Oh great," said Betty. "I have another job!"

My folks left and Betty wanted to get started taking care of Ginny. Sally took her inside and showed her where all of Ginny's stuff was.

"You'll be in charge of this," said Sally. "You'll need to get her dressed each day and keep her clothes clean. You can probably do her laundry every three or four days, but her diapers will have to be rinsed out daily. You'll have to keep her room picked up. And you can go with her grandpa when he takes her out. If you have any questions, just ask, okay?"

Betty agreed. I wondered if she could do all that, but she seemed confident and eager. And she started right in, playing with Ginny.

"You take it easy tomorrow," I told Sally. "The day after tomorrow, we'll hold a brandin'. I'll have the cook fix up a barbeque."

Sally looked relieved. She needed a rest, but would never admit it. "That sounds like a plan," she said.

The day of our branding arrived. We had all the dudes mounted and we started out to gather some cattle.

"It's good to be horseback again," said Sally. "I was beginning to think I would never get on a horse again."

"You did kinda overload yourself," I said. "In the future, we need to see if we can't get the maid staff here earlier. Missus Abercrombie was about done in even though she wouldn't admit it. And you got pretty tired. Even Jim was draggin' a little. We might want to look to hirin' some older people from town, like I did when Ginny was born."

"We'll look into that possibility," said Sally. "Right now, let's gather those cattle and hold a branding."

I was sure my comments about getting the maid staff here earlier in the year fell on deaf ears.

We gathered cattle and corralled them. Bud, Ginny, Missus Abercrombie, and Betty arrived in the four-wheeler shortly after we corralled the cattle and while Dwight and Chuck were building a fire. Betty was driving.

"Your sister drives pretty good," said Bud, "but she's a little slow. There's lemonade in the four-wheeler."

I was amazed that Bud had let Betty drive the four-wheeler.

"That's fun," said Betty. "It's not much different than Dad's tractor."

"Have you ever driven one of those before?" I was a little concerned. After all, that was my daughter she was driving around. I started to voice some concern, but Sally stopped me.

"They'll be all right," she said. "Daddy will keep her slow."

The irons were getting hot. "Sally, why don't you an' Dwight start ropin'? We need to get started before the dudes drink up all the lemonade. The cook will be here with the barbeque before we know it."

Sally roped her first calf and dragged it to the fire. I thought, *Even a pregnancy doesn't slow her down.*

Dwight was having trouble catching a calf but he finally managed to catch one. "I'm kinda out of shape," he said, as he dragged the calf to the fire. But he was smiling.

Dwight got a few calves caught then I had him and Chuck switch. Chuck had a little more luck catching calves than Dwight. Sally was catching more than anybody, but she was getting tired. I asked her, "Do you want to let Pat catch a few?"

"That might not be a bad idea," she said. "I am getting a little tired."

"Pat," I said, "get your horse. It's your turn."

I asked the dudes, "Do any of you want to try to rope a few calves?"

Their response was negative. "It looks too hard," said one guest.

"I'll rope a few then you can get the rest," said Pat.

Pat and Chuck roped calves until the cook showed up. We took a break to eat, then I started roping.

Before I started, Sally said, "Maybe Betty would like to rope. Can she rope?"

"I don't know," I said. "Ask her."

"Do you want to rope a few, Betty?"

"Sure," said Betty.

"You can use my horse," said Sally. "But remember, that's a catch rope, it doesn't know how to miss. Don't be letting it develop any bad habits!"

"I'll try," said Betty, getting on Sally's paint horse. Sally adjusted her stirrups to fit Betty and Betty rode into the cattle.

I missed my first throw at a calf and Betty gave me a good harassing.

"Let's see you catch one," I said.

Betty threw a loop and caught a calf. She dallied up like she'd done it before and dragged the calf to the fire. The guests enjoyed watching my little sister show me up.

I caught a calf and dragged it to the fire. As I passed Betty as she was headed out to catch another calf, I asked her, "When did you learn to rope?"

"Since you've been gone, I've had to fill your boots. Daddy says I'm almost as good as he is."

"Your dad would say something like that," I said.

Betty roped another calf and I missed another one, much to the delight of my sister. She was enjoying harassing me about my roping skills and I was a little embarrassed and proud at the same time. The guests took more delight in my missing the calf.

I caught a calf and dragged him to the fire.

"You're little sister is a pretty good roper," said Pat.

"She's outdoin' me today," I said. "She didn't used to be that good. I think she's had a good teacher an' a lot of practice."

Sally spent the rest of the afternoon holding Ginny outside the corral watching Betty and me rope. I was painfully aware when I would miss a calf and Sally would say to Ginny, "Oh, look! Your daddy missed another one!" or "Your Aunt Betty caught another one!"

It occurred to me that I was being harassed not only by my little sister but also my wife. I was glad Ginny didn't talk yet—the harassment might have been threefold. And the guests appeared to be joining in on Sally's and Betty's side.

We got the calves branded, counted the cows and turned them out. I was satisfied with the days work. Sally was talking to Ginny over by the four-wheeler with Bud. Betty was making preparation to drive Bud and Ginny back to the ranch. I was about to admonish Betty about driving too fast with Ginny in the outfit, but Sally beat me to it.

"You just take your time going home," she told Betty. "There's no rush, regardless of what my daddy says."

Betty nodded her head in agreement.

"And Daddy," said Sally turning to her dad, "don't you be goading her into going faster. She's just learning how to drive this thing."

"Yes, Daughter," said Bud.

They drove off, slowly. I watched them go and wondered, *How long will this last?* Sally put her stirrups back to where they fit her. We got the dudes on their horses and headed back to the ranch.

At supper that night, Bud was bragging up Betty's driving skills. "She's pretty good with that four-wheeler," said Bud. "She doesn't take the bumps too hard."

"Until Honey checks her out thoroughly on that, I don't want her taking it out without you, or Honey, or me," said Sally. "Do you understand that Betty? And, Daddy, you show her how to use the two-way radio."

"Certainly," said Betty.

"Of course, she can go every time Ginny and I go," said Bud. "She can drive. That will free up Dwight for other work. Of course, I'll take Dwight when I go fishing."

Betty liked the idea of driving Bud around in the four-wheeler and I saw her eyes light up when he said it.

"You remember, Betty, your job is to be a nanny for Ginny. We didn't bring you here to chauffeur Bud around." I tried to be stern with my little sister.

An Old Folks Home

The next few days were spent moving cattle around with the dudes. The two-year-old colts we had started were coming along well and we were riding them out on our dude rides. I made sure we had a wrangler on a good broke horse every time we took one or more of the colts out. I didn't want to take any chances. Sometimes those colts were unpredictable.

Bud divided his time between cleaning the corrals in the Skidster and riding around in the four-wheeler with Ginny, with Betty driving.

Betty was enjoying her summer. Watching Ginny wasn't such a hard job and driving the four-wheeler was fun for her. Betty even seemed to enjoy saddling Einstein and taking care of the other kids. When she watched the other kids, she would generally receive a good-sized tip from the parents. Every now and then, Sally would stay and watch Ginny and on those days, Betty would come riding with us.

The summer was slowly progressing; it was the middle of June. We had guests arriving and leaving on a weekly basis.

Ginny was about seven months old and making some sounds. Her mother assured me she was talking, but I couldn't understand her.

"If she's talkin'," I said, "it ain't English. Maybe she's goin' to be bilingual."

Sally just laughed. "You'll be able to understand her before too long. Just listen."

We held another branding and a few of the dudes wanted to rope. We let them try, but they didn't have much success. Sally's roping was as good as ever and Betty, although she had done well at our first branding, struggled a little. She was having a hard time catching calves. I did mention something to her about it, but didn't rub it in too hard—she was only twelve.

Dwight was riding his mustang mare quite often and he'd leave her colt at the barn. The colt was becoming real gentle and getting a lot of petting and brushing from the guests' kids.

Pat and Chuck were having a good time with the dudes. Bud was taking a few people out fishing; Sally was getting a lot of riding time, and making reservations for the remainder of the summer and the following year. Betty was staying busy with Ginny and didn't seem to be getting bored. Missus Abercrombie was content to spend her time either riding with us on the shorter rides or sitting on the porch.

As far as I could tell, the summer was progressing as expected. We were keeping the dudes busy if they wanted to stay busy and the hired help seemed to be content. When Sally gave one of the maids a day off, generally once a week, they would usually join us on our horse rides.

Bud had the corrals pretty well cleaned with the Skidster. He cleaned the horse pen at least once a week. One day he started out on the Skidster saying, "I've got a special project in mind. I'll be gone most of the day."

Sally asked, "Do you have a radio?"

"Yes, Daughter. I'm fully equipped. I'll call if I need you. Betty, you take good care of Ginny while I'm gone."

"Yes sir," said Betty. "Ginny, are you going to miss your Grandpa Bud?"

Betty had started calling Bud "Grandpa Bud" when Ginny

was around and soon had everyone calling him Grandpa Bud, even Sally and I. Bud liked the idea and didn't object.

On a short ride that day, Missus Abercrombie fell off her horse. She was unconscious. Sally got to her before I did.

"I don't know what's wrong," said Sally. "I don't dare move her. Call Betty and have her bring out the four-wheeler. The cook can keep an eye on Ginny for a little bit."

I did as instructed and told Betty where we were. "Come as fast as you can, but be safe! Missus Abercrombie has been hurt an' we need you."

Soon we saw Betty driving the four-wheeler through the sagebrush. She was driving fairly fast, but careful to slow down as she bounced over the sagebrush. By the time Betty arrived, Missus Abercrombie had regained consciousness.

Sally asked, "What happened?"

"I don't know. I just got dizzy and passed out."

"Are you hurt?"

"My head hurts," replied Missus Abercrombie. She had a gash on her forehead and it was bleeding profusely. I gave Sally my neckerchief to try to stop the bleeding. "My shoulder also hurts," continued Missus Abercrombie.

"Can you get up?"

"I think so."

Missus Abercrombie struggled to her feet with Sally's help. I felt sorry for the old lady as she was in obvious pain.

"Betty has brought out the four-wheeler," said Sally. "We'll take you back to the ranch in it. Can you get in it?"

"I think so," replied the old woman. "Give me a hand." Missus Abercrombie got in the four-wheeler.

"Betty, you drive us back," said Sally, "but go real slow. Honey, you lead my horse back. Pat, you lead Missus Abercrombie's horse. I'll probably take her to town to the doctor's and have this checked out."

When Betty, Sally, and Missus Abercrombie reached the ranch, Bud was already there. He'd heard my call to Betty on the two-way radio.

"I'll take Virginia to town," said Bud. "Sally, you better come along. Betty, you take care of Ginny."

"Yes, Grandpa Bud." The reply came from both Betty and Sally.

Missus Abercrombie objected strongly to going to town. "I'll be all right," she said. "I just need a little rest."

"Virginia, don't argue with me. You're going to town!" Bud was very adamant.

They were just leaving the ranch when we arrived with the dudes. I unsaddled Sally's horse and turned him loose.

There was a great deal of concern about Missus Abercrombie among the guests. I didn't know the answers to all the questions they were asking. All I could say was, "We'll know when they get back."

Sally and Bud returned after supper that night, but without Missus Abercrombie.

Bud was bombarded with questions from the guests regarding Missus Abercrombie. "Virginia is being kept at the hospital for a few days for observation," said Bud. "I'll have to go pick her up when they call. She'll be all right, she's a tough old bird. But don't tell her I said that!"

The next few days were regular routine with the dudes, moving a few cows around and doing scenic rides. Bud returned to his special project with the Skidster. He didn't tell anyone what he was doing, his only comment was, "I'll let you know when I get done."

Bud went to town to get Missus Abercrombie when they called and took Sally and Ginny with him. Ginny had a doctor's appointment the following day and Sally called her doctor and had Ginny's appointment moved up so she could save a trip to town.

Without Ginny to watch, Betty didn't have anything to do and she came riding with us. Sally had suggested she take the day and rest but Betty refused. On the ride, I questioned Betty about this.

"Don't you want some time for yourself? You should rest a little. You're up in the mornin' about the same time I am an' you hit the sack about the same time. You're bound to be a little tired."

"I'm all right," said Betty. "Dad says a change is just as good as a rest. Besides that, Ginny isn't that hard to watch and she's fun. And when I'm driving Grandpa Bud, he's watching Ginny."

"You mean you're having fun doin' this job?"

"Yes," said Betty.

"Maybe we ought to reconsider what we're payin' you for doin' this," I teased. "If you're havin' fun doin' this we're payin' you too much. Work ain't generally supposed to be fun."

Betty took me serious. "I told Sally I'd do this for free when I asked for the job. Besides that, I'm making some money watching the other kids."

"Now I know we're payin' you too much," I said.

Betty had an answer for me. "You check with Sally about that."

Betty knew Sally wouldn't reduce her wages. I knew she wouldn't either. My attempt to have a little fun had failed. My little sister wasn't as gullible as I thought she was.

Bud, Sally, Ginny, and Missus Abercrombie returned later that day. Everyone was pleased to see Missus Abercrombie and I think she was pleased that everyone made such a big fuss over her, although she objected. When asked what the problem was, she just replied, "Just something to do with low blood sugar. I'm sure old age has got more to do with it than anything else. I have some medication to take. I'll be all right."

"Honey," said Bud, "I want you to come with me tomorrow. I have something I want to show you and a special project in mind."

The next day I went with Bud in the four-wheeler. He'd built a road for the four-wheeler to the family cemetery plot. That was his special project.

"I need a gate built into this enclosure so I can drive the four-wheeler up to the gravesite. I need it to be able to open and close from the four-wheeler."

"I think we can do that," I said. "A system of pulleys an' ropes should do it. I'll bring out Dwight an' tell him what we want. He's pretty handy with that kind of stuff. Chuck can help him if he needs it. He should be able to get the pickup up here with the equipment he needs. When do you want it done by?"

"There's no rush," replied Bud. "I just need it done. I've been used to coming up here to reflect and think some and have missed it since I've been confined to the wheelchair or four-wheeler."

The next evening after we'd completed our tasks with the dudes, I took Dwight out to the cemetery plot and explained to him what Bud wanted.

Dwight surveyed the situation. "I think we can rig something up," he said. "Let me think on it a day or two and I'll have a list of the supplies we'll need. It should only take a day to do it."

A day later, Dwight came to me with a rough sketch of what he had planned and a list of the supplies he needed.

"We'll pick up this stuff next time someone goes to town," I said. "As soon as we get it, you can get started."

"I can get some post holes dug and plant the posts now if you want," said Dwight. "Then all I'll have to do is rig the pulleys and hang the gate."

"You just do what you need to," I said. "You're in charge of this project. You can start on it anytime you want. But you need to get it done fairly quick so we can use you with the dudes. We've got dudes leaving an' more comin' in next week."

Dwight got started and in one day he had everything set up. All he needed was the pulleys and ropes.

We scheduled another branding the following week and it went well. Missus Abercrombie didn't ride out with the dudes, but she rode out with Bud, Betty, and Ginny in the four-wheeler. The old gal didn't want to be left out of anything. They always brought lemonade and it was always appreciated by the guests. The cook was doing a barbeque every time we held a branding.

Betty got a chance to rope and her roping improved from the last time she'd roped. My own roping was just about like it had always been, but I was able to out do my little sister. Sally was the best. It seemed like she never missed a loop.

A few of the dudes wanted to rope and we let them. Although most of them couldn't catch anything, it was fun watching them try. Occasionally when one of the dudes caught something, they would have trouble making their dallies. But a lot of them were game to try.

We moved cattle around, not only to keep the dudes busy, but to keep up with our pasture rotation system. The guests thought it was great, as they had a chance to do some actual cowboy work. But I thought we were missing something and I didn't know just what it was. We'd stayed on top of our cattle work and quite often we'd take the dudes out when we'd ride fence. I was becoming concerned that we were missing something and asked Bud about it one evening.

"I don't think there's anything else we can do," said Bud. "The guests seem to be satisfied and happy. That's being shown by the number of reservations Sally's taking. She's already filled up a lot for next year. We just need to keep doing what we've been doing. Just keep it safe. So far, Virginia's the only one that's fallen off her horse. That's a good average."

"But I kinda feel like we should be doin' more," I said. "I just don't know what it is. We're goin' to have to have somebody watch Missus Abercrombie all the time if she goes out ridin' with us."

Bud laughed. "When you figure out what it is, you let me know! Don't you worry about Virginia, I'll take care of her. She can go with me in the four-wheeler if she wants to go out."

The summer wore on. Bud kept Missus Abercrombie busy with him, Betty kept Ginny with her either in the four-wheeler with Bud or busy with the other kids and Einstein. They did a lot of pony walk rides for the kids.

Pat, Dwight, Chuck, and I stayed busy with the guests. Sally helped out with the guests when she could and she took care of the phone and reservations. Jim and the three maids took care of the housekeeping chores. The whole outfit seemed to be running well, just as expected.

Bud called me in one day to talk to him. "When do you want to hold our second horse sale?"

"I haven't given it any thought," I said. "Pat thinks the spring is best, it's not so hard to get the colts lookin' good when they're sheddin' their winter coats. They might bring more money in the spring."

"We're pretty busy in the spring and short-handed at that," said Bud.

"I think we could do it about the first of May, for one day."

"Then we'll shoot for the first of May. I need to start making up a sale catalog. You figure out what horses you want to keep, we'll need a few for our dude string, and let me know. That means we won't have any weaners to sell, just yearlings and two-year-olds."

In July, we had a lot of rain. The guests didn't ride in the wet weather, but we still ran in the saddle horses every morning. The moisture was welcome and the rains made the country look greener. The grass got a boost and it was welcomed.

One morning, we had a good steady, soaking kind of rain. The ground was soaked. We were bringing in the saddle horses. I was riding one of the two-year-olds and he slipped on the wet ground. We went down. The horse landed on my right leg. I couldn't tell if I had cleared my stirrup, so I kept the horse's head turned around so he couldn't get up. I didn't want the horse to get up with my foot in the stirrup and perhaps get dragged. I also had a pain in my right shoulder, the same one I had hurt in the rodeo a few years earlier.

Pat saw us go down and immediately rode over to us.

I asked, "Can you see my foot? I can't tell if I've cleared the stirrup! I can't move my foot."

"I can't tell," said Pat. He was off his horse. "Give me your mecate. We'll let him up easy. If you're hung up, I'll keep him an' we'll free you."

I didn't like the idea of letting the horse get up not knowing if my foot was in the stirrup or not. I had to trust Pat completely.

Sally rode up and held Pat's horse. "What happened?" She asked the question although the answer was obvious.

Pat let my horse get up, keeping a close hold on his head. The horse struggled to his feet. My foot was clear of the stirrup although my toe was still in it and I felt a sharp pain in my leg when it fell to the ground. Pat led my horse away and the horse had a noticeable limp.

I tried to get up and found that I couldn't. I thought I had broken my leg and it was quite painful. Sally saw that I couldn't move. She gave Pat his horse and said, "I'll come back with the four-wheeler."

"Bring a rifle with you," said Pat.

"It ain't that bad," I said, trying to be funny. I looked over at the horse I had been riding. Pat was unsaddling him and he was standing without any weight on his right front leg. His leg was dangling below the knee—it was broken.

Sally left at a fast gallop. "You be careful," I yelled after her. "It's slick out here!"

Sally just waved her hand in acknowledgement as she rode away. Chuck and Dwight had followed the saddle horses in and when Sally got to the corrals, she handed her horse to Chuck, saying, "Take care of my horse. Honey's been hurt! Just proceed with things like normal, get the horses saddled for the dudes."

She didn't answer any questions, but went straight to the lodge. She got a rifle from Bud, saying, "Honey's been hurt."

Bud asked, "Is it that serious?" His attempt at humor fell on deaf ears.

Sally got the four-wheeler and came out to where I was stranded. I had managed to sit up while she was gone although it was quite painful. She handed the rifle to Pat and took his horse.

Pat took the gun and put the paint colt out of his misery. A bullet between his eyes did it quickly. Pat took my hackamore off the colt and put it in the back of the four-wheeler with my saddle.

Pat and Sally had to help me up and I managed to get in the four-wheeler. "Do you want to ride back with us?"

"No," said Pat, as he got on his horse. "I really feel safer on my horse, an' I think I'll make better time."

Pat trotted off toward the corrals and Sally and I started back in the four-wheeler. She drove real slowly, but it was a painful ride to the barn. Pat had beaten us back to the ranch. Sally drove right to the company car and with Pat and Dwight's help, I managed to get in the car.

Bud was there in his wheelchair. "If you tell me where the colt is, I'll go bury him with the Skidster while you're gone. You just take all the time you need. We'll handle everything here. Oh, by the way, you'll miss breakfast!"

Sally drove me to the hospital and the ride to town was easier than it had been in the four-wheeler. Sally drove right up to the emergency entrance to the hospital, and the hospital staff helped me onto a gurney and wheeled me into the hospital. I managed to get my chaps off. Sally parked the car and met me inside. They were taking X-rays when she came in.

The doctor showed up looking at the X-rays. He put them on the light box and showed them to me. "There's nothing broken," he said. "It appears like it's a strained ligament. We'll have to cast it and it will probably take longer to heal than if it was broken. We'll do that now and you can be on your way. You'll need to stay off it for a few days and you'll be on crutches, probably about a month or so, maybe longer."

"I've never heard of a pulled ligament bein' put in a cast," I said. "Sally, while they're castin' this, you better go get somethin' to eat. You've missed your breakfast."

"I can't," said Sally.

"How come?"

"In the rush, I forgot my purse. I don't have any money. I don't even have my driver's license."

I reached in my back pocket and got out my wallet. I gave Sally some money. "Get something to eat an' get me a new pair of jeans. They've cut these ones up pretty good. I'm glad I took off my chaps an' gave 'em to you before I came in here."

"Do you want me to bring you something?"

"Yeah," I said.

"What?"

"Anything," I said, "I ain't really that hungry."

Sally left and they put my leg in a cast and provided me with a pair of crutches. When they were done, I sat in the waiting room waiting for Sally to return. When she arrived, a little old lady, a nurse, wheeled me out to the entrance. I felt embarrassed to be wheeled out by this little old lady, I really felt like I should be wheeling her! I didn't have a chance to put on the new jeans Sally brought me.

I got in the car with some difficulty, and ate the breakfast Sally brought me while we were driving back to the ranch. Because my leg was in a cast, I had to sit close to Sally, where she generally sat when I was driving, with my right leg stretched out across the right side of the front seat.

"Well," said Sally, as she put her right arm around me, "it appears that there are some fringe benefits that are coming along with this accident. This might be all right after all!"

"Both hands on the wheel," I said. "You don't have your driver's license, remember?"

"I'll take my chances," said Sally, laughing.

"This is goin' to make it kinda tough on everybody. I won't be able to be of much help, bein' laid up."

"I think we'll manage," said Sally. "What does Daddy say, 'When the going gets tough, the tough get going,' or something like that."

"Yeah, but I don't know what I'll be able to do."

"You won't have to do anything," said Sally. "Just listen for the phone and take reservations. We're pretty much full, but you can always work on next year. And you can spend more time with Ginny and Betty. You just need to take it easy and get better. I'll do your job."

I didn't know if I liked the idea of my wife doing my job, but I wasn't in a position to argue. I knew Sally, Pat, Dwight, and Chuck could handle everything, but I didn't like the idea of being left out.

Talking on the way home, I made the comment to Sally, "With Bud in a wheelchair, Missus Abercrombie needin' pretty much constant attention, Ginny needin' a babysitter, an' me on crutches, the Wilson Ranch is fast becomin' an old folk's rest home! I don't know what we're goin' to do."

Sally laughed. "But we're still making money!"

"Just what are you goin' to charge me for a month or so of just sittin' around?"

"I'll give it some thought," said Sally. "We might be able to arrange for a discounted rate! We'll have to see."

A Slow Time

When we arrived at the ranch, everyone was gone except Bud, Missus Abercrombie, and the cook.

"Do you folks want something to eat?" The cook was concerned.

"No," I said. "We had a late breakfast. I think I can make it until supper. Where is everybody?"

"They're all out riding," said Bud. "Even Betty is out with Ginny in the four-wheeler. They'll all be back in an hour or two."

"Is Betty all right in the four-wheeler?" I was still a little dubious about my little sister and the four-wheeler.

"Yes," said Bud. "She's a very careful driver, especially since Virginia made such a big deal out of her coming out and saving her life when she fell off her horse. She's very conscientious. Don't worry. I got the colt buried earlier today. I'll have to delete him from our sale catalog."

"You need to get some rest," said Sally. "The doctor told you to stay off your feet."

I didn't see how I needed some rest as I hadn't done anything all day. I wasn't tired. But I did lie down on the couch. I didn't have anything to do and quickly became bored. *A month of this will kill me,* I thought.

Bud asked me, "Where are you going to hide?"

"What do you mean?"

"I mean, where are you going to hide? We need to keep you out of sight. On those crutches, you can't be good advertising for us!"

I just laughed.

The next month was boring for me. Because I'd hurt my shoulder in the fall, I couldn't really get around too well on the crutches. It was quite painful. But I could ride in the four-wheeler with Ginny and we spent a lot of time driving around in it. Betty would put Ginny in the car seat and we'd go out to the branding corrals when there was a branding and watch.

Often, Betty would ride out horseback and she really looked forward to her turn at roping. Occasionally, I would let her ride Roman or Drygulch.

One day while Betty was putting Ginny in the car seat, I asked her, "How much are you goin' to pay me for doin' your job takin' care of Ginny for you?"

Betty's reply was a question. "How much are you going to pay me for doing your job? Somebody has to keep these dudes in line."

It was a standoff. I couldn't tease my little sister.

"You know," I said, "you're not supposed to take advantage of me while I'm laid up! You keep that up an' I'll tell Mom on you!"

"You just go ahead and tell her," said Betty. The only person finding any humor in my comments was me.

It was the first part of August when I finally got the cast off. My leg was weak from not being used but I thought I could get back in shape fairly fast. I walked with a noticeable limp for a while and after my first attempt to get on a horse was a little painful, I used the mounting block to get on a horse. I took a lot of teasing from everybody using the mounting block, especially from my little sister. It was embarrassing, but it was good to be horseback again. I really thought I was any man's equal when I was on a horse.

My roping certainly hadn't improved while I was in the cast and I missed quite a few throws at the first branding I went to after getting out of the cast, much to the delight of Sally and Betty. I still felt a little pain in my shoulder from the horse fall. I was taking a lot of teasing from both of them. But it was all done in fun and we managed to get all the calves branded.

Since I could get back on a horse, Betty had been relegated back to driving the four-wheeler with Ginny and Bud. I had spent a lot of time watching Ginny and enjoyed it. Betty was really a good hand with the cattle considering her age, but she didn't mind going back to her principal job—that of watching Ginny. And she was helpful in watching Bud and Missus Abercrombie.

Things were getting back to normal, although I was still hobbling around. I had to be pretty careful when on foot in the horse corral or the branding corral. I couldn't move as fast as I used to. Pat, Dwight, and Chuck had done a good job while I had been out of commission.

While there wasn't anything pressing to do, other than move a few cows around and take the dudes on scenic horseback rides, it was still good to be horseback. Dwight and Chuck had been riding the two-year-old colts on a regular basis and my horses, Roman and Drygulch, had gotten a good rest, other than when Betty rode one of them.

My leg had gotten better and I didn't have to use the mounting block to get on my horse. My shoulder still hurt occasionally and I thought I might have it checked next time I went to town. But it didn't hurt enough to where I couldn't do my job.

We finally got all the calves branded and our horseback rides were mostly scenic ones. We'd go out and ride fence occasionally, but we'd done that so much the fences were in good shape. It was just an excuse to convince the dudes we were doing something worthwhile.

One morning we noticed a horse missing after we'd run in the saddle horses.

Dwight asked, "Where's the big paint of Sally's, the one Bud gave her?"

"I don't see him," I said. "I'll go out an' look for him. He's got to be out there somewhere."

"I'll go with you," said Dwight.

"You'll miss breakfast," I replied.

"That's okay. This is more important."

"That's up to you," I said, "but let's get goin'."

When we reached the horse pasture, we split up. "Stay pretty close to the fence," I said. "You'll be able to look over a larger area. If you find him an' there's anything wrong, give out a long, hard holler. I'll do the same."

About twenty minutes after we split up, I heard Dwight yelling. I hurried over to where his yelling was coming from and saw Dwight, down in a holler, off his horse and kneeling on the head of the big paint horse. The paint was on the ground. From the looks of things, the paint had got a wire caught between his hoof and his shoe, struggled trying to free himself and went down. There was no telling how long he'd lain there. I couldn't see Dwight's horse.

I got my pliers from my saddlebags and cut the wire. The big paint got up, painfully, and limped around. He had a noticeable limp in his right front leg.

"How long do you think he's been hung up there?" asked Dwight.

"I dunno," I said. "He's put up a pretty good struggle judgin' from the way the ground's dug up. Where's your horse?"

"I didn't tie him up. I suppose he went back to the ranch. The paint, he wasn't fighting when I first saw him," said Dwight.

"He probably pooped himself out before you got here,"

I said. "We'll have to take it easy on him. His foreleg is hurt, looks like up in the shoulder, an' he's pooped himself out fightin' the fence. We'll probably have to call the vet when we get to the ranch. You bring him slowly an' I'll go on ahead an' help with the regular chores. I'll pull that shoe when you get to the ranch. Take your time, you're afoot anyway."

I gave Dwight my lariat rope to lead the horse back. "Make sure I get that rope back," I said. "It's a catch rope, not a throw rope!"

"Not all the time," replied Dwight, laughing. He'd seen me miss my fair share.

I gave Dwight a dirty look and started back to the ranch. I met Sally coming out to look for us.

"When Dwight's horse came to the ranch alone," she said, "I came out to look for you. I thought something might have happened. Where's my horse?"

I told Sally what happened to her horse. "You might want to call the vet, I don't know how serious it is."

Sally became very worried and called the vet as soon as we got back to the ranch. I went to help with saddling the dudes' horses. Dwight would miss the dude ride, but if he was nice, he might be able to talk the cook out of something to eat. I changed horses and went on the ride with the dudes.

When we got back from the dude ride, the vet was just driving up to the lodge. Dwight had gotten back with the big paint and had put him in a stall in the barn.

I helped get the dudes off their horses then went to the barn to see what the condition of the big paint horse was. Bud and Sally were already at the barn helping the vet.

The vet was examining the horse. He was pushing against the right shoulder of the horse. He did it a number of times. Satisfied, he had Sally lead the horse around.

"As near as I can tell," said the vet, "there's nothing broken. I would guess he's strained a ligament or some muscles. Keep him separated, out on pasture if you can. It might take a few weeks for him to recover, but he should be all right. If he gets worse, give me a call. I don't think we will have to, but we might have to put him down if he doesn't show some improvement. Keep plenty of this liniment on him, it might help."

Sally's reaction was mixed. She was hopeful the horse would recover, and be useful, but dismayed that he might have to be put down. "We'll do whatever we have to do to make it right with him."

"So, Bud," said the vet, "how are you feeling?"

"Probably better than that horse," replied Bud. "At least I can move around as free as this wheelchair will let me. Come up to the lodge, have something to eat and relax a little. I'll introduce you to my granddaughter. She's a lot of fun."

"I'll just do that," said the vet. "We can figure out when you want to preg check."

Bud and the vet went to the lodge. Sally instructed me to go to the laundry room and get some old towels, which I did. When I returned with the towels, Sally soaked one of them in the liniment and applied it to the horse's shoulder. I pulled the horse's shoe.

"We won't need to reshoe him until he gets better. You're goin' to smell just like horse liniment for a few days," I said.

"That's all right," replied Sally. "I really don't mind the smell of horse liniment."

"But what will the dudes think of it?"

"We'll just tell them it's western perfume. They'll get used to it."

"It's pert near as expensive as perfume," I said.

I helped Sally give the horse a good rubdown with the liniment then we turned the horse loose and went to the lodge for the noon meal.

Bud informed me when he and the vet had decided to preg check and asked, "Is that date good for you?"

"It should be," I said. "I'll have to put it on the board in the office. I'm gettin' so many things to do I can't keep track of 'em unless they're written down. Sometimes I feel like nothin' more than a secretary."

"Don't feel like that," said Bud. "You're mighty important to this outfit. Somebody has to keep it all together."

"While we're figurin' out these dates, let's get a few more figured. We need to figure out when to gather cattle an' wean the calves. We'll need a few days to gather, a few days to sort, a day to hold the calf sale an' a day or two, maybe three to ship. Once we get done with the cattle, we'll need to gather the broodmare band an' wean the colts. I also need to figure out when Betty's got to go back to school—right before Labor Day, I suppose. I'll need to make arrangements to take her home or have my dad come out an' get her."

"You have your dad come and get her," said Bud. "We'll be pretty busy around Labor Day. Make sure Sally has a room reserved for them. Betty has sure been a big help around here. I think it would be a good idea if she came back next summer."

We got all the dates marked on the board. To look at the board it appeared like we would be pretty busy. We still had guests coming in after Labor Day. But the dudes could help with the cattle and that would alleviate a lot of the chores. And Chuck and Dwight were handy. And of course, Pat was always there.

Satisfied that we had all the bases covered, I asked Sally to call my folks and see if they could pick up Betty before Labor Day.

A Family Reunion

Sally called my folks. Apparently they were already planning on coming out to pick up Betty. A date was made when they could come and get her back to school on time. The date was a little early, as Betty thought she had to do some shopping for school.

As August wore on, the nights started getting a little cooler, the days shorter, and the number of dudes dwindled. Many of the dudes had timed their vacations so they could get back home and get their kids in school. The pressures of running a dude ranch became less and the job became more enjoyable, although just riding around on sightseeing trips was becoming boring to me, even though the dudes seemed to enjoy it. I was actually longing for a little more excitement.

One day Pat came to me and said, "Honey, I'm thinkin' we ought to take a day or two an' check our broodmare bunch."

"Why?"

"I dunno," replied Pat. "I just got a funny feelin'."

"We'll be gatherin' them in about a month or so. Do you think it's necessary to check them now?"

"It might not be necessary, but it might be prudent."

"Well, Pat," I said, "I've been a little bored lately. That might be a good idea. Chuck an' Dwight can handle the dudes, there ain't that many here. It might be good to break the routine."

"Better bring a bedroll, just in case," said Pat.

I gave Pat a strange look. "What's up?"

"Nothin' that I know of," replied Pat. "I just got a funny feelin'."

"I'll get a bedroll an' some groceries. You thinkin' we'll need a packhorse?"

"Might not be a bad idea. I'll get a packhorse saddled while you get some food. Don't forget the plates an' utensils. Don't forget the coffee an' cream an' sugar. Last time I did this, I forgot the coffee an' I had a miserable camp. Make sure you get somethin' good to eat an' be sure to get somethin' to cook it in. What horse do you want to ride?"

"Roman, I guess. Drygulch has been used pretty much lately."

"Better bring enough for two nights," said Pat. "I don't know what we'll run into out there."

I had no idea what Pat's premonition was and couldn't figure out what he had in mind hard as I tried, as I headed to the kitchen to get the groceries. I told the cook what I needed and he got it together while I got my bedroll. It had been some time since I used it, and unbeknownst to me, Sally had washed it.

I told Sally and Bud what Pat had in mind and that we might be gone two nights and three days. Bud got a funny look on his face.

"Last time Pat had one of these kind of feelings, our broodmare bunch had wandered close to forty miles off their range. It took him and me pert near a week to find them and bring them home," said Bud. "You pay close attention to him. It might be a wild goose chase but if Pat thinks something's wrong, there probably is."

Sally asked, "You want me to go along, Honey?"

"No, Darlin'. You better stay here an' keep this place runnin' right. I don't know what would happen if you were gone for a few days."

"Dwight and Chuck can handle things here," said Sally.

"I know. But I'd feel better knowin' someone is here that really knows what's goin' on."

"But I don't know what's going on out *there*," replied Sally.

"I don't either," I said. "But I'll find out an' you'll be the first one I'll tell when I find out." I gave Sally a goodbye kiss, picked up Ginny, gave her a kiss an' told her to be good. As I left, I told the cook I'd be up with the panniers to pack the groceries.

When I got back to the barn, Pat had his horse saddled and was just finishing saddling the packhorse. He'd picked a mare from the dude string for a packhorse.

"What'd you get her for?" The mare he'd picked wasn't particularly fast.

"She'll keep up," answered Pat. "An' if she falls behind, she'll catch up, eventually."

"I'll take the panniers up to the lodge after I saddle my horse an' pack the groceries."

"I'll load the horses in the two-ton truck an' meet you at the lodge," said Pat.

I loaded the panniers as even as I could weight-wise and was ready to go when Pat brought the truck to the lodge. Another kiss for Sally and we were off.

Pat drove the truck as I pumped him full of questions about where we were going and just what we were going to do. I didn't get any definite answers, Pat just kept saying, "We'll find out when we find out."

We drove about forty miles from the ranch before we stopped. Pat got a set of binoculars out of the truck, stood on the running board and glassed the countryside.

"Nothing!" he said. "Not a thing!"

"What are you lookin' for?"

"Horses, mostly. Plus anything else that shouldn't be here."

We drove another forty miles or so before Pat stopped again. He got out but this time he didn't get the binoculars.

"There," he said, pointing to the ground in front of the truck. "Horse tracks!"

"Yeah," I said.

"You don't see?" said Pat. "Those are shod horse tracks over unshod horses. Somebody's pushin' horses somewhere."

"Where?"

"I don't know," said Pat, "but I got a pretty good idea."

He got back in the truck and we started following the tracks. I didn't know how he could follow the tracks driving the truck, but he did. We bounced through the sagebrush for a mile or so, and then he started looking for a smoother way to travel.

"I think I know where they're headed. There's an old road over here, I'll play a hunch an' head for it."

"I'm sure glad you know the country," I said. "I ain't never been in this part of the country before."

"You ain't lost, are you?"

"Not yet," I said. "I can still find my way home."

"That's good," replied Pat. "We might become separated. I'd hate for you to get lost."

"I'd be all right, if I had the groceries. The cook gave us plenty."

"That's good. We may be out here longer than what I figured."

Presently, we came to the old road.

"I hope my hunch is right," said Pat, as he pulled onto the old road and picked up speed. Another ten miles or so down the road, we came upon a cowboy riding a bay horse. He stopped when we approached.

Pat stopped the truck. "Where ya headed?"

"There's twelve or fifteen cows an' calves 'bout a quarter mile ahead of me. They strayed a little far an' I'm takin' 'em home."

Pat's eyes immediately glanced to the road ahead of him. Satisfied, he asked the puncher, "Seen any horses around here?"

"Yeah," replied the cowboy. "There's a bunch over that ridge." He pointed to a ridge off to the west. "I followed 'em for a while, but never did get close enough to see any brands on 'em. There's a lot of paints in the bunch an' it looks like all the colts are paints. I figured 'em for rangs. They could belong to that Wilson Ranch up north—they're supposed to be runnin' some paints. But they're a long way from home if that's whose they are. I was goin' to put the cows where they belong then come back an' see if I could get close enough to see if they was branded."

"We're from the Wilson Ranch an' we're lookin' for our broodmare bunch."

"That might very well be the horses you're lookin' for," said the cowboy. "There are corrals up this road about another mile or two. If you want, I'll take care of the cows then help you corral 'em."

"That won't be necessary," replied Pat. "If they're the right ones, we're fixin' to take 'em home."

"That's got to be 'bout a hundred miles or so," said the puncher. "I ain't never been up that way."

"It's quite a ways," said Pat. "Mind if we leave the truck at the corrals while we take our horses home? We'd be back for it in a couple of days."

"That's okay with me. It'll be all right, I've got a camp right there by the corrals."

"Thanks," said Pat. "That's what we'll do."

Pat started the truck and we headed down the road. Soon we came upon a dozen or so cows and calves.

"That's good," said Pat. "Leastways he was tellin' the truth about the cows."

"You don't think he was lyin' to us, do you?" I'd kept pretty well quiet during the conversation with the puncher.

"I didn't know," said Pat. "You can never be too sure."

We arrived at the corrals, unloaded the horses and packed the packhorse. Pat took the lead rope to the packhorse and we headed out.

"With a little luck, we'll get ahead of the horses. It shouldn't be too hard to turn 'em an' start 'em home. We'll let 'em take us home, as long as they're headed in the right general direction, we'll just follow."

"Sounds good to me," I said.

We located the horses and I could tell they were our broodmares as I recognized some of them. Pat still had the packhorse so I turned the horses to the north. The stud came out to meet Pat, and Pat pulled the halter off the packhorse and turned it loose. The stud herded the packhorse to the broodmare bunch.

"You just lost our groceries and bedrolls!" I'd gotten the broodmares turned in the right direction and had ridden back to meet Pat.

"Nope," said Pat. "That stud will keep the mare up with the others an' we won't have to drag her along. She's easy to catch an' we can get her when we want to make camp. Let's hurry them along some, we want to get them a little tired so they won't stray too far at night."

"I'll get ahead of 'em an' try to get a count on 'em," I said as I left.

"Good idea," replied Pat. "I'll just follow along an' keep 'em movin' at a good trot."

I rode my horse out around the broodmares and got ahead of them where I could get a good count as they went by.

When Pat showed up, following a good distance behind the stud, he hollered, "How many did you get?"

"I ain't sure," I said. "I only get twenty-three an' I think there's supposed to be twenty-four, if I remember right. I'll get ahead of 'em an' count 'em again."

"Twenty-four is what's supposed to be there," yelled Pat as I left. "Twenty-four mares an' one stud!'

I got ahead of them again and counted the mares. This time I was sure, twenty-three mares. We were missing one!

"I get twenty-three again," I said as Pat rode up. "I'll count 'em again, just to make sure." I rode off and I heard Pat muttering something about, "How many times do you have to count 'em to know how many there are?"

I laughed to myself as I rode away. I thought, *This time I'll count the colts, just to make sure. If we're missin' a mare, we're probably missin' a colt, too.*

I got ahead of the broodmare bunch and counted the colts. When Pat got to me, I said "We got a problem."

"What's that?"

"We got twenty-three mares an' twenty-four colts. We're missin' a mare," I said.

"That is a problem," answered Pat. "You sure?"

"I counted the mares twice, an' I'm pretty certain I got a good count on the colts. You go count 'em if you want."

"Naw, your count's good enough for me. I wonder where she is. That ol' stud wouldn't let a mare slip away an' get lost. Something has happened."

We hurried the broodmare bunch along, careful not to get too close to the stud. We kept them going at a good trot and when we reached a small creek, we decided to stop them and make camp for the night. They were ready to stop and we figured they'd graze around the creek and settle down for the night. We didn't know if we'd convinced them they were headed home but hoped they'd gotten the idea. I went to gather up some firewood while Pat caught the packhorse.

I found a lot of firewood and dragged it to where Pat was unpacking the packhorse. The broodmare bunch was grazing toward the north, in the general direction of the home ranch.

"I guess we can camp here," said Pat. "This place is as good as any."

"Suits me," I said, as I unsaddled my horse and hobbled him. "What can I do to help?"

"Get a fire goin' while I unsaddle an' hobble my horse. We'll have somethin' to eat here right directly."

"Did you pack an axe?"

"Yeah," answered Pat. "There's a hand axe in one of the panniers."

I dug through the panniers until I found the hand axe and started a fire. Pat brought out the cooking utensils and groceries.

"Good thing the cook sent frozen steaks, they ain't even thawed out yet! Looks like he sent plenty," said Pat. "You want corn or corn with your taters?"

"Corn. We don't need the steaks thawed out, they can thaw while they're cookin'," I said.

"Right," said Pat. "Get some water for coffee an' we'll be set. Bring enough so we can wash the taters, we'll cook 'em an' eat 'em with the skins on."

"Are you sure that's civilized?"

I took the coffee pot and went to the creek. I returned with a full pot of water. I split the water into two pans and went back to the creek for another pot of water for the coffee. When I returned, Pat had cleaned the potatoes and had them frying up with the steaks. The corn was cooking in the extra pan.

After supper and a couple of extra cups of coffee, I took the pots and pans to the creek and rinsed them off. I brought back plenty of water for coffee in the morning. Pat walked around the broodmare bunch.

When he returned, he said, "Your count's right. Twenty-three mares an' twenty-four colts. One of the colts has lost his mom an' I think I know which one, but can't be sure. We'll know better in the mornin'."

"When we get closer to the ranch, we maybe ought to catch him an' bring him in closer to home," I said.

"That's not a bad idea. He's big enough to be weaned an' would probably be all right, but closer to home would be better."

I asked, "Which mare do you think is missin'?"

"I ain't sure," said Pat. "Bud knows these mares better than I do, he'd be able to tell once he saw all of them. But I got an idea."

We visited until right after dark then hit the bedrolls. The night was clear, there were a lot of stars out, and off in the distance I could hear a coyote howl. I fell asleep thinking, *How could it be better than this?*

The next morning, Pat was already up and had a fire going. "You goin' to sleep all day?"

"It wouldn't bother me," I replied.

"Coffee's 'bout ready. Our saddle horses are close an' the packhorse is with 'em. We'll be up an' goin' before too long."

"I'll gather up the horses," I said.

We had steak for our morning meal, saddled the horses, and packed the packhorse. Before we headed out, I took a couple of cans of stewed tomatoes out of the panniers, gave one to Pat, and put the other one in my saddlebags.

"Lunch," I said.

"You're getting soft," said Pat

We came across the broodmare bunch about a mile from where we had made camp. It looked like all the horses were there. I thought I ought to get a count on them, but Pat said, "It ain't necessary. That stud won't let anybody wander off."

We moved the mares about the same as we had done the day before, at a good trot. Around noon, we ate the stewed tomatoes while moving the horses.

"That was a good idea, Honey," said Pat, as he tossed the empty can into the sagebrush.

"I thought you might like it," I said. "I've noticed you seem to be gettin' a little soft an' I think us younger generation needs to be a little more considerate of the older generation."

"It's about time I started gettin' some of the respect I truly deserve," replied Pat.

This good-natured bantering continued throughout the trip—it helped to relieve the boredom.

Toward evening, we made camp alongside a creek and the second night was pretty much like the first night.

The following day, the country started to look a little more familiar. We were getting closer to home.

"We've got about two more days before we can turn these horses loose," said Pat.

"How's our groceries holdin' out?"

"We should be all right," replied Pat. "We might get a little hungry 'cause we're out of steak, but the cook put a few cans of beans in there. That should hold us."

"I wonder how things are goin' at the ranch," I said.

"Things are most likely good there. Ain't much that can go wrong this time of year."

"I know," I said, "but I'm still concerned."

"Don't be too concerned," said Pat. "You've done a good job managing this outfit the last couple of years an' Bud an' Sally are surely capable of making management decisions. Nope, I wouldn't worry too much."

Around noon on the third day we noticed some buzzards making big lazy circles off to the northeast of us.

"I got an idea what that's all about," said Pat, "I think I'll ride over there an' check it out."

"That's a good idea," I said. "An' while you're at it, you can bring that colt back that's wanderin' off in that direction."

"That sorta confirms my suspicions," said Pat.

He rode over in the direction of the buzzards. Shortly, he returned leading a spotted colt. He'd fashioned a halter out of his lariat rope and was halter breaking the colt as he returned. The colt seemed willing enough, but would occasionally balk. It was part of his education.

"My suspicions were confirmed," said Pat. "This colt was hangin' out where his ma had died. Havin' a small family reunion. It'll be the last time he sees her."

"I had a hunch," I said. "What mare was it?"

"The oldest mare in the bunch, this colt's mom. Let's catch up the packhorse an' fish out the halter. We'll let the packhorse continue to educate this young feller."

I caught the packhorse and we haltered the colt and tied him to the pack saddle. The packhorse could continue to teach the colt how to lead.

"We'll have to keep an eye on 'em," said Pat.

"Any idea on what killed the mare? Any predator signs?"

"Not what I could see," answered Pat. "I figure she's been dead about four or five days. The coyotes ain't even got to her yet. She was pretty old, probably died from old age. Bud had told me he was thinkin' of sellin' her an' was havin' a hard time choosin' between sellin' her an' just lettin' her live out her life here."

"Well, he don't have to make that decision now," I said.

"Nope."

We made camp that night and it was pretty much like the previous nights. We lacked the luxury of steaks and dined on beans.

The next morning we saddled up and packed the mare. I roped the colt and much to my surprise, he didn't hit the end of the rope hard. The mare had done a good job of teaching him how to lead.

"That's one we don't have to halter break this winter," I said, as I led the colt to the packhorse.

"But we still have to teach him to be respectful around humans an' that we ain't goin' to hurt him. With a little luck, we should reach the home ranch before dark tonight."

"I think we'll put this colt in with Sally's grulla. It might not be a good idea to mix him in with the saddle horses an' he might be good company for Beauty," I said.

"We maybe ought to turn these broodmares loose closer to home," said Pat. "Maybe they won't wander off."

"We'll leave 'em on water," I said. "I'm thinkin' they wandered 'cause the waterhole dried up."

"You're probably right," said Pat. "Tomorrow we can take the dudes out an' check the waterholes on their range. Somebody's gonna have to take someone an' drive the two-ton truck back."

"Do you want that job?"

"I don't much care," replied Pat. "Can you find your way back to the corrals where we left the truck?"

"I think so," I answered. "I'll go an' get it with Dwight or Chuck, if you don't feel up to it."

I sensed that Pat didn't particularly look forward to retrieving the truck.

"I'm certainly up to it," replied Pat. "But I'd rather stay in the saddle. If you're goin' to go an' get it, I'll draw you a map so you don't get lost."

"That's just what I'm beginnin' to think," I said.

"What's that?"

"I'm thinkin' that the only job of management is to do all them things you can't get the hired help to do!"

"You might be right," laughed Pat. "Yep, you might be right at that! But you're doin' a good job of doin' those things!"

I thought Pat had paid me a back-handed compliment, but didn't answer back. A prolonged discussion about how well I was managing this outfit might become embarrassing. Sometimes I felt like I wasn't measuring up.

We reached the home ranch after leaving the broodmares on a shallow creek. We caught the packhorse and colt to lead them back to the ranch. Tomorrow, after Pat checked the waterholes, we might have to move the horses to a different range. As we rode into the ranch, I noticed a new pickup parked in front of the lodge. *More dudes,* I thought.

Pat and I unsaddled our horses and the packhorse and turned them loose. I took the colt to the pasture where Sally's grulla was pastured and turned him loose.

I was surprised to see my parents and my brother inside the lodge. A small family reunion was held, although my mother was fairly busy holding Ginny. They'd arrived the day after Pat and I'd left and had waited a few days to see me.

"We've come to take your nanny back for school," said my dad.

"Is that your new truck parked outside?" I asked.

"Yep," he answered. "Just picked it up. This trip is its break-in drive. Tommy gets the old one."

With the broodmares wandering off, I'd forgotten about Betty having to leave. That would mean Sally would be busier not having anyone to help with the baby.

We visited for a while and Pat told them about finding the orphaned colt and bringing him home. Pat described the dead mare to Bud and he knew her well.

"Betty," I said, "you've done a good job with Ginny this summer, although I tend to think you've got her good and spoiled. It'll probably take all winter to undo the damage you've done with her!"

"Honey," said Sally, "don't talk like that! Betty's done a real good job!"

I could see my dad smiling at my comment. Apparently he was the only one that had seen any humor in my comment.

I got a piece of scratch paper from the desk and started to do some figuring. When I finished, I looked at the paper and said, "Betty, it's time we settled up. I've figured your wages, and then subtracted your room and board, the charges for your horseback riding, and I come up with a figure of one hundred and twenty dollars you owe us!"

"What?" Betty's look was incredulous.

"That's right, one hundred twenty dollars!"

My dad, Pat, and Bud were laughing, my mother was grinning but strangely silent, and Betty was still looking at me in disbelief. Sally was amazed.

"You can't treat your sister like that! She's done a really good job," said Sally.

Betty said, "I told you I'd do it for nothing. If you're going to pay me a wage, then deduct room and board and horseback riding, I'd just as soon forget the wages."

"If we forget the wages, then you'll owe us more to cover the charges," I said. "You eat like a horse. You'd best take the wages."

Sally was becoming agitated. I winked at her to let her know I was only kidding.

"If you want," I volunteered, "you can come back next summer and work off what you owe us. Of course, you might want to bring your own groceries, just to cut down on your expenses."

"I'm not so sure I want to come back, if you're going to charge me to work for you," said Betty.

Betty's comment brought a roar of laughter from my dad, Pat, and Bud. Mother was even trying to control her laughter and Sally was having a hard time controlling hers.

"I think it's time you stopped tormenting your sister," said Sally. "She's done a good job and deserves an honest wage for her work."

"Well," I said, "I guess so. You write her out a check after supper and make sure it's for enough that she'll want to come back next summer. Let's go eat."

Betty's face showed a sign of relief and we went to eat supper. We only had two guests staying at the ranch and they expressed a great deal of inertest in riding out to check waterholes the next day. Pat assured them it would be a long day in the saddle but they wanted to go anyway.

After supper, I tried to assure Betty that I was just joking about her owing us money for her work during the summer. She wasn't too sure of my intentions and I became positive that she didn't have much of a sense of humor. I told my mother to make sure she understood I was only joking on the way home tomorrow.

The next day, we did the morning chores, saddled up two horses for the guests and Pat, Dwight, and the dudes went out to check the waterholes. I said goodbye to my folks and Betty and they left for home. Betty appeared to have gotten over her feelings being hurt and even said, "We'll see you at Thanksgiving."

"Thanksgiving?"

"Yes," replied Betty. "Mom and Sally set it up. You're coming home for Thanksgiving."

That's all she said and they left.

I took Chuck in my old pickup and went to bring the two-ton truck home.

It was an uneventful drive to the corrals where we left the truck, and uneventful back. We got back to the ranch in the middle of the afternoon, before Pat and the other riders showed up. I figured they'd get in around dark.

Sale Day

The riders showed up shortly after dark. They'd had a long day in the saddle, but their ride had been successful. According to Pat, the waterholes were dry, but they'd located the broodmare bunch and put them in another pasture that didn't have any cattle in it, but it did have water.

The dudes liked the idea of rounding up the horses—it gave them a sense of doing some real cowboy work.

The following day, the dudes left. The ranch was vacant except for the people that worked there. It was kinda nice, real peaceful. Some of the cabins were winterized, although it seemed a little early.

Sally explained that there were only a few reservations for the fall and we would save money closing some of the cabins now. "Besides that," she said, "with Betty gone and the maids having gone back to school, I can't take care of them and Ginny too. Your sister was a big help around here, even if you don't know it."

"We could hire that woman from town, like we did awhile back," I said.

"We don't have that many reservations," answered Sally. "With what hasn't been winterized, I can handle that and take care of Ginny at the same time. I think it's asking too much of Daddy and Missus Abercrombie to watch Ginny every day. We won't lose anything and the bottom line tells me that this is the best year we've had in a long time, so far. It might be the very best, depending on what we can sell the calves for."

"I hadn't given the calf sale any thought," I said. "We'll have to look on the board an' see when we've scheduled it for. We need to have enough cabins to hold the buyers."

"Daddy's already taken care of that. He notified the buyers while you and Pat were out looking for the broodmares. We have enough cabins and rooms available. He's doing the same thing as he did last year—charging those people rent that don't buy anything. I suppose some of them won't come back. I think some of them are just looking for a free place to stay for a couple of days."

"But more buyers push the price up," I said.

"If you look at the records, the same cattle buyers are buying the cattle each year."

"Records?"

"Yes," replied Sally. "There's a complete set of records for each year going back to when Daddy started this place."

"Really? I was unawares."

"Oh, yes," said Sally. "They don't get used much, but they're there just in case. It's a real accurate record of this ranch. Just like a history. If you want, I'll show you where they are so you can look at them."

"I'm not too interested in lookin' at a bunch of figures about what cattle were sellin' for years ago."

"But there's more than just figures in it. It reads like a history and there are a lot of side notes about what was happening at the time. I'll set some of them out, if you're interested, you can look at them."

"Okay," I said. But I was sure I wouldn't be too interested.

The next few weeks passed peacefully. There were a few guest check-ins, mostly older retired folks and a few young married couples. We started gathering cattle in preparation for weaning and selling the calves. We took the dudes with us if they wanted to go when we gathered cattle. There were some long days and a lot of the dudes weren't up to riding the next day.

At the end of each day, we'd separate the calves from the cows and at the same time sort the steer calves from the heifers. The longhorn calves were easy to tell and we sorted them from the other calves. We were making preparation for our annual calf sale.

Bud had spent a lot of time in the Skidster cleaning corrals and hay had been delivered from the valley below. We were almost ready for winter. We'd still have to go through the heifer calves and pick the heifers we wanted to keep for replacements.

Our calf sale day was fast approaching. We had some guests staying a little longer than they had indicated and we had to open up one of the cabins we had already winterized. Sally didn't seem to mind, "It improves the bottom line," she said.

She wouldn't let me hire a woman from town to help her out. I was concerned she might be doing too much by herself, but she assured me that Missus Abercrombie was a big help.

I didn't think Missus Abercrombie was much help. She was fairly old and even I could see she was slowing down. Concerned, I volunteered to help.

"We can handle this," said Sally. "It would be harder to have to work around you if you tried to help."

"But I could take Ginny an' that might help."

"No," said Sally. "Daddy wants to take her as much as possible. He's even strapped the car seat permanently into the four-wheeler. We have everything under control. You make sure everything goes well at the calf sale."

The cattle buyers started arriving a couple of days before we'd scheduled the sale. The hunting season had passed and we had refused a lot of hunters permission to hunt. We'd posted the complete outer boundary of the ranch. The few guests we had got quite a workout riding with Chuck and Dwight with the "no trespassing" and "no hunting" signs as they nailed them to the fence posts every half mile or so.

Everything was ready for our calf sale. I accompanied each buyer into a corral as they looked over the calves. Pat would accompany another buyer into a separate pen, then the buyers would meet with Bud and dicker out a price. Bud couldn't go in any of the pens due to his being in a wheelchair.

I didn't really care for this arrangement; a lot of walking was involved. The buyers would try to pump me for information about what had been offered by other buyers and what Bud would accept, but I wasn't any help to them.

I was really glad when the day was over. I'd been on foot all day, accompanying the buyers through the corrals full of steers. Pat had taken the buyers through the pens that held the heifers. After we got done with the steers and heifers, Pat took those buyers through the pen of cull cows we had and I took the buyers through the pen of Longhorn cross calves. We had a few bulls to sell and the buyers looked at them from outside the corrals. Even though this was a dude ranch, the bulls hadn't seen a man on foot for quite a while and we didn't want anyone to get hurt.

The cattle buyers were making their offers to Bud. I don't know how he kept track of everything, but he seemed to be in control. Those cattle buyers that weren't successful left dejectedly and those buyers whose bids Bud accepted made arrangements for their trucks to come and to stay an extra night. I figured we'd have a busy day the next day, loading the cattle. But it would mean we'd have fewer chores to do in the future.

Trucks had arrived during the night and we got an earlier than usual start in the morning.

The next day, Pat, Dwight, Chuck, and I saddled horses to move the cattle to the loading chute. We'd had enough of the footwork. Besides that, we hadn't wanted to take the cattle buyers into the corrals horseback, it would have taken too much time—getting them on and adjusting the stirrups.

The day after, we still had cattle to load but by noon we'd moved the calves off the ranch. We had a few truckloads of cows to load and move out and a load of bulls. By suppertime all the sold cattle was gone.

We still had a few guests at the ranch, but by the end of the week our tourist season would be over with. I thought that would be all right. Ginny's first birthday was fast approaching and I thought it would be proper to have a family birthday party for her, although I wasn't sure she would understand what was happening.

A few weeks after the last guests had left, we celebrated Ginny's first birthday. I found it interesting that she seemed to enjoy the wrapping and the boxes that the gifts came in more than the gifts themselves. She got the stuff a one-year-old would normally get if she lived on a ranch—cowboy boots, cowboy hat, a stick horse, a rocking horse, and a real small pair of chink chaps. Everything a young cowgirl would want if her parents were horse people. Missus Abercrombie was the only person that gave her something that didn't have anything to do with the ranch and our activities on the place. She gave her a doll, dressed in city clothes. It appeared that Ginny liked that gift better than any of the rest, as she took it everywhere she went. Missus Abercrombie was real proud that Ginny appeared to favor her gift more than anyone else's. "The young girl needs to grow up to be a lady," she said, "and I'm just helping her!"

Ginny was walking, or rather running, everywhere she went. I found it very humorous to watch her. I watched her while Sally closed up the remaining cabins for the winter. Jim, the head housekeeper, had stayed around long enough to help close up and winterize the cabins. Missus Abercrombie had decided to spend the winter, "just to help with Ginny," she said. "And to make sure she's raised like a lady. We can't have her being raised by a bunch of barbarians."

Sally asked, "You mean to say I'm a barbarian?"

"No," replied Missus Abercrombie, "certainly not! But this little girl needs to be raised as a lady and have a real chance at life."

"But she can grow up out here and still be a lady," said Bud. "Much the same as you are Virginia."

Missus Abercrombie was taken aback a little by Bud's comment. She didn't know what to say, and thankfully remained silent. But she was determined to stay the winter at the ranch.

Secretly, I was pleased with her decision. With her willing to watch Ginny on occasion, Sally would have a little more time to herself. And she needed that.

More Feed

Snow came in November and by Thanksgiving there was more than a foot on the ground. I was beginning to think we might have to start feeding earlier than usual, but Bud took the Skidster out and plowed some paths out on the more level parts of the pasture where the cows were kept.

"Windbreaks," he said.

But I suspected that he was thinking we might run a little short of feed by spring. I questioned him about this later.

"You think we might ought to get some more hay up here before too long?"

"It might not be a bad idea," he replied. "I guess I could call Fred. He'll have some extra."

"Fred?"

"Yes, you know my brother Fred. He runs the farming part of this operation."

"I didn't know there was a farming part to this operation," I said.

"Oh, yes," answered Bud. "Fred runs the farming part of the business. He's got a bunch of help that run the farm while he's out doing his game warden job. We've been buying our hay from him for years and he delivers it. He sells hay to Rod, my other brother, and Rod winters his sheep on the farm. At one time this was all one business—cattle, sheep, hay, and grain. Just about the biggest ranch in the state when it was all together. Each one of the ranches is still pretty big. When my dad died we split the ranch three ways; I took the cattle end of it and expanded into horses and eventually dudes, Rod took the sheep, and Fred got the farm out in the valley. Each one of us brothers got the part he was most interested in. I wasn't particularly interested in the sheep or the farm. If you notice, there isn't any irrigation on this outfit. I really hate irrigating."

"A man after my own heart," I interrupted.

Bud laughed. "I could see that from the start! But," he continued, "Rod took the sheep because he liked the idea of two cash crops each year, wool and lambs. I like the idea of two cash crops a year, that's why we got the dudes. When we added the registered paint horses about twenty years ago, we added a third cash crop.

"Fred got the farm, although his interests lie more in wildlife. But he's got a good crew; some of his hired help are descendants of some of the people that worked for my dad. I'll call Fred tonight and see if he's got some more hay. I'd rather have too much than not enough going into the winter."

"I'd feel better with more hay," I said.

"You've really taken quite an interest in this place, haven't you, Honey?"

"Of course," I said. "I'd sorta planned on makin' this my home."

Bud laughed again. "For your information, it is your home!"

"I'd sorta figured that when Sally didn't charge me room an' board when I'd hurt my leg last summer," I replied.

Bud was still laughing. "Remind me to talk to Sally about that!"

"I should have kept my mouth shut," I said.

Bud called his brother later that night and made arrangements to have more hay delivered when the roads were suitable.

"I'll have to plow out a spot where we can put it," said Bud. "We'll need to store it where the elk and deer can't get to it. Our regular stackyards are pretty full."

"I've given this some thought," I said. "We could build a new stackyard out by the feed ground, on that piece of sagebrush ground above the creek. We'd just need some tall T posts and net wire. We'd need a set of gates that is tall enough that the elk an' deer couldn't jump over. It shouldn't be too difficult."

"The ground's already pretty well frozen solid," said Bud.

"We can rent an attachment for the Skidster that will pound the posts through just about anything," I said.

"We'll do it," said Bud. "You better come to town with me tomorrow and make sure we get the right attachment. I'm not sure I know what we need."

"You sure you just don't want to be chauffeured into town?"

"No, Honey. You're in charge of this operation, you need to come along just to make sure we get what you want."

Bud overlooked my attempt at humor. I could tell he was serious about this.

"Maybe you ought to come with me to see where I've got this planned," I said.

"I know the spot," said Bud. "I'll have to take the Skidster up there and plow it out. We don't want to be working in a couple of feet of snow."

The next day, we went to town in my truck to get our fencing supplies. We had a problem renting the post pounder, as the company wanted to rent the equipment attached to a Skidster, but we just wanted the post pounder. We ended up taking the Skidster with the machinery attached, at a discounted rate. I had to call the ranch and have Pat bring the two-ton truck to haul the Skidster to the ranch. I had the net wire, clips, and steel posts in my truck. I also had some plastic tarps we'd use to cover the hay when it arrived. Pat would have to haul the gates back with the Skidster.

Dwight and Chuck would have to handle the evening chores by themselves, but they had done it enough in the past that they knew what to do.

When Pat arrived, we loaded the Skidster and headed back to the ranch. It was after eleven o'clock at night when we got back and we decided to wait until the next day to unload everything.

The next morning, after we did the morning chores, we unloaded the Skidster and post pounder from the two-ton truck. Bud arrived in our Skidster and started plowing snow from what was to be our new stackyard. We'd left the wire, steel posts, and clips in my truck; we didn't want to have to dig them out from under any snow. I also got a bag of fence staples and a hammer and a couple of two by fours to stretch the wire.

I measured off the size of our stackyard, just a little longer than a semi trailer and a little wider than three times the width of a semi trailer. I added a few feet on each side and the ends so we could stack the hay away from the fence. I didn't want the hay so close to the fence that the deer and elk could push against it and get to the hay. Enough heavy pushing would weaken the fence and eventually they would be in the stackyard.

We set the corner posts and braces, and then stretched some baling twine tight between the posts. Even though it was cold, I wanted a straight fence. I was careful to show Bud where the baling twine was laying on the ground. He was pushing snow and a lot of sagebrush a good distance from where our stackyard was. It was kinda nice—we had snow-free and sagebrush-free ground to work on.

Halfway through laying out the stackyard, I changed my plan. Originally I had planned to just have a set of gates on one end but decided to put a set of gates on both ends. This way the semi truck could drive straight in, we could unload the hay from each side, then the truck could drive straight through when we had unloaded it. We could do the same thing when we loaded the hay to feed. It would mean we'd have to set some more posts to hang gates on and get two more gates, but I figured we could get the gates when we returned the Skidster. I liked the idea and when Bud saw that I was modifying the original plan, he waved me over and asked, "What you doing?"

I explained how I'd changed the plan because it would make it easier to unload the hay when it arrived. I didn't mention the fact that we wouldn't have to carry each bale of hay any farther than necessary when we loaded and unloaded the hay. He thought about it for a minute, nodded his head in approval and went back to plowing snow.

Pat, Dwight, and Chuck had already started pounding steel posts about every ten feet. I'd stepped off the distance and marked the ground where the posts were to be set. Pat was running the Skidster, Chuck was holding the posts in place until they got started good and Dwight was driving the truck and unloading the posts at the marked spots on the ground.

As I finished marking off the spots where the steel posts were to be set along the baling twine, Bud drove up.

"This is a pretty smooth operation we've got going here," he said.

"Yep," I said as I admired how smoothly the work was going. I was pleased. "We should have this done by tomorrow, then take the other Skidster back, pick up the extra gates an' be ready to take in hay. When will it be here?"

"Fred told me he could have it here the first part of next week."

"That's good," I said. "When is that?" I'd lost track of time and didn't even know what day of the week it was.

"Today is Thursday," replied Bud. "It should be here by Tuesday. Did you lose track of time, Honey?" Bud was smiling.

"I'm afraid I did," I answered. "I ain't so sure I need to know what day it is anyway. As long as we can get everythin' done when it needs to be done we're right on schedule. Soon as Pat reaches the corner, I'll roll off some wire an' start rollin' it out. We might be able to stretch wire this afternoon. We'll be done with this project before we know it. It won't bother me none, it's plenty cold out here. How you holdin' up in the cold?"

"I'm all right," said Bud. "I put some extra layers on this morning. How are you doing?"

"I've been walkin' enough to stay sorta warm, but it's gettin' to me."

"Here," said Bud, "have some coffee. I brought out a couple of thermoses." He handed me a thermos.

"Coffee! What do you think this is, a café?"

"Not a café exactly, but it will become a food storage area— for the cattle. Take all the coffee you want, I brought plenty for everyone. You think those guys are ready for a break?"

"They probably are," I replied. "But things are goin' so smooth, I hate to interrupt them."

"A little ten-minute break won't hurt them," said Bud. "Get in, we'll give them a little coffee."

We drove to where Pat was operating the Skidster. Pat saw us coming and stopped the operation. I think he was glad to get off the Skidster and move around. He came to us rather stiffly.

I got off the Skidster and with some difficulty, started a fire with the sagebrush Bud had plowed up. A little warming fire wouldn't hurt anything on a cold day like today was.

"It sure is cold today," Pat said, as he took the coffee Bud offered him. "I could have used this half an hour ago!"

Dwight and Chuck came up and got some coffee. Bud was right, he'd brought plenty. Everyone except Bud gathered around the fire and warmed themselves up. He drove the Skidster as close to the fire as he could get it.

"We'll have this done by tomorrow," said Pat. "The ground's only froze about six or eight inches. The posts are goin' in pretty fast an' easy. Plowin' that sagebrush away will certainly make it easy to stretch wire."

As Pat made his comment, I thought to myself, *It's nice how we all seem to think along the same lines on this outfit.*

Our little ten-minute break ended up lasting a little longer than half an hour, but it was good to take a break from the job. The warming fire was going pretty good and nobody really wanted to leave it. But the time came when we had to get back to work.

Pat didn't say anything, he just headed for the Skidster. Dwight and Chuck knew it was time to go back to work and followed Pat.

"I kinda thought we shouldn't have taken a break," I said, as I noticed their reluctance to leave the fire.

"That won't hurt anything," said Bud. "They're all good workers and they deserve it. Like you say, we'll be done with this before we know it."

"They're almost to the corner, I'd better get up there an' get the wire ready," I said.

I got to where Dwight was about ready to turn the corner and I stopped him and told him what I wanted. He helped me roll off a roll of the net wire.

"What side of the posts do you want the wire on?"

"Put it on the outside," I replied. "The idea is to keep the deer an' elk out! We don't have to worry much about the hay leavin'!"

Dwight pushed the wire to the outside of the stackyard then continued with his job. I fastened the net wire to the corner post and started rolling out the wire. I was sure glad Bud had cleared away a lot of the snow and sagebrush, as it made rolling out the wire easy.

Bud saw what I was doing, brought the Skidster over and asked, "You ready to stretch wire, Honey?"

"Soon as you get here," I answered. "Let me get this set up an' we'll get started."

I fastened the wire between the two by fours so we could stretch the wire, then hooked it onto the Skidster with a chain and Bud stretched the wire. As he stretched the wire, I walked along and pulled it up in various spots to get it as tight as possible. As soon as it was tight enough, I signaled Bud and he held the Skidster in position until I could come and staple the wire to the corner post.

When we had the wire tight and stapled to the posts, I cut the wire and tied off the ends around the post. I went to the truck, got the clips and started fastening them to the steel posts.

Dwight got done laying out the posts and came over to give me a hand. When we had the one side done, we started rolling out wire on the end. This wouldn't be such a hard pull as this was the short end of the stackyard. But it would require two pulls, one from each side, as we had to leave room for the gates.

By the time we had the wire stretched on the end, Pat and Chuck had finished pounding the steel posts and they had started rolling out wire on the long side of the stackyard.

"If we keep going like we're going, we'll have this done to-day," said Dwight.

"Not really," I answered. "We've still got to stretch more wire and that will be a little more time consuming than what we're doing now."

"How come?"

"This is a stackyard, built to keep deer an' elk out," I replied. "We need to stretch this net wire above the wire we've already stretched. Then the wild critters won't be able to jump in."

"Oh! I'd lost sight of what we were doing."

"That's all right," I said. "Just keep doin' what you're doin' an' we'll get done eventually. We've done pretty good today, but we're goin' to have to go to the house soon. We still have the evening chores to do."

"Yeah," said Dwight, "I'd almost forgot them."

Dwight's comment was one of those things that slipped out without thinking. I'd made plenty of comments like that, without thinking, and I remembered how stupid I felt after I'd made them. I decided not to tease Dwight about it.

We got the other long side of the stackyard stretched and decided to go back to the ranch to do the chores. As we headed back, I thought about what we had to do tomorrow—stretch the one end, then stretch a span of net wire above the wire that was already up and hang two gates. I got to thinking I'd need to bring a ladder out so we could fasten the wire to the steel posts. I'd need to get two more gates in town when I took the Skidster back and they'd need to be hung, and then we'd have our new stackyard. We wouldn't get it done tomorrow, it would be the next day, but that would be soon enough.

The next day, after we got the morning chores done, we went to the new stackyard and stretched the wire above the bottom. Bud didn't come out, as he couldn't do much being confined to a wheelchair. We used the Skidster to get the wire to the proper height, and then used it to fasten the clips to the steel posts. I'd forgotten to bring the ladder. It was a slow, time-consuming job. After a lunch break, we completed the job.

We loaded the rental Skidster onto the back of the two-ton truck and chained it down. We'd be ready to take it back to town the first thing in the morning. Pat took the truck and I drove the other Skidster back to the ranch. Other than getting the two extra gates and hanging them, our new stackyard was complete.

The following Tuesday, the hay came right on schedule. Fred didn't come, but he'd sent two helpers along with the driver to help unload the hay. With Pat, Chuck, Dwight, and myself and Fred's hired help it didn't take long to unload the semi trailer.

"Two more loads this size an' we'll have this stackyard full," said Pat when we were done. "I sure like your idea about leaving the center open, it sure makes unloadin' easier."

"It'll make it easier to load it, too," I replied. "We'll cover it when all of it has arrived."

"The next load will be here day after tomorrow then two days later the last load will arrive. Think that'll be enough?"

"I hope so," I answered. "Bud told me that was all Fred had left. He needs to keep some for the sheep that Rod winters there."

During the time we had been building the stackyard and unloading hay, Sally had been keeping up her doctoring of her grulla, Beauty. He started showing some improvement and he actually started playing with the orphaned colt Pat and I had brought back from the desert. Sally kept giving him the treatment, even though he was showing signs of improvement. She thought a lot of that horse.

She told me one night, "I'll probably keep his treatment up all winter if necessary."

"Do you think it'll take that long? Why don't you call the vet an' see if it's goin' to be necessary?"

"It's expensive to have the vet come out here," she answered.

"It can't be more expensive than that liniment you're usin'."

"The horse is worth it," she replied.

"The only thing wrong with him is his name," I said.

"And what's wrong with his name? He's a beautiful horse."

"That's true," I said. "But the name Beauty just don't set good with me."

"Well, that's his name and I ain't … ah, I'm not changing it. I swear, you're ruining my English! Are you sure you're not a bad influence on me?"

The first of December arrived and it stayed cold. In fact it got colder. We stopped using the horses to ride through the cattle, it was too cold. We'd give them a good looking over when we fed. I needed a horse to use getting the sick heifers out of the feedlot, and it was miserable riding in that cold. We installed a heater above the squeeze chute to prevent the medicines we were using from freezing. It was the coldest winter I could remember.

My folks invited Sally, Ginny, and I for Christmas, but we declined. We, in turn, invited them, but they declined. We were all too busy taking care of our chores to get away.

Bud, Sally, and Missus Abercrombie handled the Christmas shopping chores. Pat, Chuck, Dwight, and I supplied lists of what to get everyone and they did the shopping and wrapping. Pat and I took some extra time one day and cut a Christmas tree and took it to the lodge. As cold as it was, we were still going to have a Christmas.

Christmas that year wasn't too exciting. Everyone got extra layers of warm clothing. It was appreciated and put right to use. Ginny was the only one that got anything to play with. I was kinda disappointed—I'd always wanted an electric train and didn't get one. That was all right, we didn't have time for me to play with it if I'd have gotten one.

Jokingly, I said to Sally, "I didn't get an electric train."

"Did you want one?"

"Yes," I said. "I've wanted one every year since I was eight years old."

"Why didn't you say something?"

"I thought it might be considered kinda childish," I replied.

"That's all right," said Sally, "Christmas is a time for kids and it's okay for adults to act like a kid, occasionally, during the holidays."

"I didn't know that," I said, as I took a candy cane off the Christmas tree and peeled the wrapping off it.

"But that doesn't mean you can eat the tree decorations!"

The new year came and there wasn't much celebrating at the Wilson Ranch. The cold was beginning to have an effect on everyone. I think everyone was wishing for an early spring.

One night Bud said, "We generally get an early thaw in January. I'm ready for it now. It wouldn't bother me if it came tomorrow and stayed until April!"

"I'm all for that," said Pat. "This cold weather is gettin' to me. We've got enough snow to provide all the water we need for next summer."

"What are you complaining about? I've been stuck in that kitchen every day and it's toasty warm," said the cook. "I haven't noticed any cold."

"I'd almost trade jobs with you," I said.

"Don't even think about it," replied the cook. "If you started cooking, none of the hired help would stick around and the dudes would be few and far between this summer."

"You're probably right," I said.

"He is," said Bud. "When the January thaw comes, it'll get better."

But the January thaw didn't come and it continued to stay cold. Just doing the daily chores became a real chore. We'd decided to put off halter breaking the weaner colts until the weather became nicer. Occasionally, I'd have to saddle a horse and bring in a sick cow for doctoring. Even though Pat, Chuck, and Dwight volunteered to do this, I thought it was my job as a boss and I didn't want to take advantage of my position and stay where it was warm.

I'd take the sick cows to the feedlot where I could doctor them with the advantage of having a heater so the medicine wouldn't freeze. While I had the horse saddled, I'd ride through the replacement heifers. I got miserably cold and often I'd have to get off by the fence because I couldn't feel my feet, and I'd have to use the fence to keep my balance. At the end of the day, I'd get to the lodge and soak my feet in a pan of warm water. I think my feet were getting frostbitten. Pat, Chuck, and Dwight would generally doctor the cows while I rode through the heifers.

When February came it was still bitter cold, in fact it was frigid. Chuck had come down with pneumonia and Sally took him to town. He spent a few days in the hospital, and our chores became harder, missing one man. Bud placed an advertisement in the local paper in town, but nobody responded. No one wanted to work out in the cold.

When Chuck returned from the hospital, Bud suggested he only work half days. Bud thought the cold might have an adverse effect on his health. Chuck insisted he was all right, but Bud prevailed and Chuck was only allowed to come out and drive while we were feeding.

I was beginning to become worried. Calving season was fast approaching and the newborn calves would have a difficult time as cold as it was. I was beginning to dread the approaching calving season. In anticipation of calving season, we ran in the saddle horses and began riding them. As cold as it was, the horses didn't appreciate being saddled and ridden, but it was a necessary chore.

I'd been using my horse, Roman, all winter and thought I'd give him a couple of months off when calving season started, so I saddled Drygulch. I really expected him to buck pretty hard when I climbed on him, but he just took one jump and walked right out. I was surprised. I knew he was a good horse, but maybe he was better than I'd thought. I picked another horse to use for calving season, one of the paints we had started the previous year and started to ride him. We didn't have a problem.

Pat got his personal horse saddled and ridden without any problems and picked another horse to use during the calving season. He didn't have any problems with either horse.

Dwight was another story. His little mare didn't like the cold weather. She bucked him off three times in a row. The third time Dwight hit the ground, he didn't get up as fast as he had the previous two times. Chuck and I had to help him up. He was hurt, not badly I hoped, but he was done for the day. We got Bud's four-wheeler and took him to the bunkhouse. He tried to assure us he was all right, but we thought differently. He was hurt and he couldn't walk.

The cook went to the bunkhouse, checked out Dwight and suggested we take him to the doctor. He'd busted his hip in the past and thought Dwight had done the same thing. Sally and Bud got Dwight loaded into the back seat of the car, much against his objections. They returned later that night without Dwight. The doctor had suggested they go straight to the hospital and have X-rays done. The X-rays revealed Dwight's hip had been cracked and it would require some time to heal. He would need to stay in the hospital for a few days and when he did come back to the ranch, he'd have to stay off his feet for a few weeks.

Chuck had picked two horses and both of them crow-hopped a little, but Chuck rode them. I was hoping it didn't go to his head; they hadn't bucked all that hard, and he really wasn't that good of a bronc rider.

We were set for calving season if we could take the cold. With Dwight in the hospital and Chuck only able to work half days, the next morning Sally joined Pat and I to do the chores. I tried to object, using all the arguments I could think of, including Ginny needing to be taken care of.

Her reply to that was, "Daddy and Missus Abercrombie can take care of Ginny. They've been doing it every day while I've been out doctoring Beauty."

I was unaware that she had continued to doctor her horse every day during the cold spell. I asked, "You're still doctoring the horse in this cold?"

"Yes," she replied.

"Why?"

"You're doctoring sick cattle every day, aren't you?"

"Sure," I answered. "But I thought he was pretty well cured."

"This will only improve his chances for a one hundred percent recovery."

I was beginning to wonder if she thought more of that horse than she did of me. It wasn't the first time I'd had these thoughts.

Sally was determined to come out and do what she could. The way she was bundled up, I wasn't sure she could do much. But she was willing to try. This only strengthened my admiration for her.

Dwight still came out and drove, but Sally pitched right in loading the hay. I was surprised how she handled it. Other than having to feed a little hay occasionally, I didn't think she'd done much work with the hay. But Sally's help did enable us to fairly well get the chores done on time.

A Reprieve

Right before we were scheduled to start calving we started to ride through all the heifers looking for those heifers that were ready to calve. I had some doubts about how successful our calving season was going to be with the cold. It might be that some calves might freeze to death before we could do anything for them. And if we had a heifer reject her calf, that might mean certain death for the calf. It was a stressful time.

Chuck and Pat started riding through the cows on a daily basis and I rode through the heifers. I was surprised when Sally showed up, saddled her horse, Beauty, and started riding through the heifers with me.

"What are you doin'?"

"I'm here to help you," answered Sally.

"I really don't need any help."

"Yes you do! If I can help a little, we'll all get done quicker. Even though Dwight's home, he can't do much. So, I'm helping."

"Are you sure your horse can take it?"

"He'll take it. I've been saddling him and riding him every day a little for the last week. I think he's okay. We'll find out."

We left our horses at the calving sheds that night so we could ride through the heifers on a daily basis.

A few calves arrived a little early. I'd noticed them "springing" and Sally and I put them in separate pens under the calving shed. They calved without my assistance and I really wished we had put overhead heaters in the sheds as I watched the calves shivering as they nursed. I made a mental note to have this done before the next calving season. I mentioned this to Bud at supper that night.

"It might be a pretty good idea to put some overhead heaters under the sheds before next year's calvin' season. It's quite a shock to those newborns to hit the cold. They're born shiverin'."

"As cold as it's been, that is a good idea," replied Bud. "I'll get on it right away."

Two days later an electrician and his helper showed up and installed heaters in the sheds. I was pulling a calf when they arrived and the helper was totally amazed. He'd never seen anything born. Sally explained to the helper what I was doing.

Soon, it started to warm up. It got warm enough that I could eliminate one extra layer of clothing. That made it easier to get on my horse, but it was still difficult. My feet were always cold even though I soaked them every night in warm water. Some of my toes were turning black. Sally noticed this and promptly told me we were going to town the next day to the doctor.

I objected, but Sally persisted. "You've frozen your feet. Gangrene could develop and you could end up having a leg amputated or even dying. You're going to town! Pat can check the heifers."

I couldn't argue much. It would mean extra work for Pat, Chuck, and Dwight, but I didn't want to end up crippled the rest of my life.

The next day, Sally and I went to town. The doctor took one look at my feet and promptly checked me into the hospital. That afternoon, I was put to sleep and a few of my toes were amputated on my right foot. I don't remember much about it other than it was the most peaceful sleep I'd had in a long time. The next morning when I woke up, my folks were in the room with Sally and Ginny. She'd called them when I went into the operating room.

"How do you feel, son?" my dad asked.

My mother was strangely silent, but she looked very serious. I was still kinda groggy. "I'm okay. I'll be able to help out in the morning. How much did they cut off?"

"They took three toes off your right foot according to the doctor," said Sally.

"Only three? I won't miss 'em. I'll be able to work in the morning," I said.

"I don't think so." It was the doctor. He'd come in the room while we were talking. "You need to stay off your feet for a few weeks and give everything a chance to heal. You'll be in the hospital for a few days before you can go home. We'll give you some physical therapy, load you up on antibiotics, get you on your feet, but you'll have to use crutches for a while. With those toes missing, you'll have to learn how to balance again. You're lucky we didn't have to take off your foot! A few more days and that would have been more serious."

"I don't know that I can do that," I said.

"You don't have a choice," said Sally. "You'll do what the doctor says."

I didn't have a chance. After some visiting with my folks and a tearful goodbye from my mother, Sally and my folks left to get something to eat. I was asleep when they returned and my folks went back to their ranch. There wasn't anything they could do.

The next day Sally was in the room sleeping uncomfortably in a chair when I woke up. Sally woke up when I stirred.

"How are you? You can't be comfortable," I said.

"I'm okay. Are you all right?"

"Why sure," I replied. "Just layin' here in bed, sleepin' durin' the middle of the day when I should be workin', in a nice warm hospital room, out of the cold, I couldn't be better!"

"Don't try to be funny," answered Sally. "You've just had an amputation. It's very serious!"

"Losin' three toes can't be serious," I replied. "I don't even remember usin' 'em."

After a prolonged discussion about how serious my amputation was, I changed the discussion to Sally's welfare. I convinced her that she should return to the ranch and take care of Ginny. My convincing argument was that "Ginny was probably raising the dickens with Missus Abercrombie and she was gettin' along in years. And Ginny wasn't used to bein' without her mom for an extended period of time."

It took some persuading, but Sally finally agreed to go back to the ranch. "I'll come and get you when the doctor calls and says you can come home. By the way, Daddy says he's glad to hear you're okay and he'll lend you his wheelchair if you want."

"Very funny," I replied, "very funny!"

A few days later Sally and Bud showed up to take me back to the ranch.

"It's a coming," said Bud, "it's a coming!"

"What's comin'? What's happenin?"

"A Chinook! We're almost done with this blasted cold weather. A few days and you'll feel it!"

I asked, "How do you know?"

"I can feel it in my bones," replied Bud. "By the way, I've hired a high school kid to help out while you're laid up."

"A high school kid! I thought you'd need at least three men to take my place! How come he's not in school?"

"He's a high school dropout," replied Bud. "He keeps getting into trouble in town. His folks thought some good, honest hard work might be good for him and I've been acquainted with his parents for quite a few years."

"Hard work never hurt anybody," I said. "But a high school dropout! I thought if you hired somebody to do my job you'd have to get someone with at least a little education! I guess I know what my worth to this outfit is!"

Bud laughed. "You're more valuable to this outfit than you realize. But Pat and the boys will need some extra help. They'll have to be checking the first calvers and shortly the cows twice a day in addition to the regular feeding chores. I plan on using him to do the simple stuff like loading the hay and helping feed. We'll have to show him how to stack the hay and the like, then after a few days we'll turn him loose on it. I'll take him under my wing and guide him. He kinda rebels at authority, but I can handle that."

"When's he showin' up?"

"Today," answered Bud, "he's in the car waiting for us. He's going back with us."

I rolled my eyes skyward. "I guess in addition to bein' an old folks home an' a recovery center for invalids, we're becomin' a wayward teenager probation center!"

Bud and Sally both laughed.

"It's not that bad," said Sally. "Daddy's always had a soft spot for the down and outers."

I asked, "Is that why he hired me?"

Again, Bud and Sally laughed.

"That's not why we hired you," said Bud. "We hired you because you were mature beyond your years and I saw something I liked there. Just as I figured, you've become an instrumental part of this outfit. You've become very important to this operation."

Quietly, I valued Bud's comments. Trying to be funny, I said, "After those comments, if you really meant them, this would be an opportune time, if I weren't crippled up, to ask you for a raise, just to help me get on my feet again!"

"You need to stay off your feet for a while, according to the doctor, so, to help you stay off your feet, your request is denied, only of course, to help you out."

This time it was my turn to laugh and Sally joined me.

Bud continued, "If you can get on your feet again, we'll consider the question at that time." Bud laughed at his own comment.

We left the hospital. I was wheeled out of the hospital in a wheelchair pushed by an older nurse. I felt like I should be pushing the nurse out in the wheelchair, rather than her pushing me. The new help, the high school dropout had brought the car to the front of the hospital and was waiting for us.

"I'll drive us back to the ranch," said Sally, as she approached the driver's side of the car. "Put Daddy's wheelchair in the trunk."

I noticed a look of distaste on the new help's face, but he obediently followed Sally's instructions. I got into the front seat of the car and Bud and the new hand got into the back.

"If I'd have had a younger woman pushin' me out of the hospital, I'd have challenged you to a race," I said.

"You wouldn't have won," said Bud. "I've always enjoyed having the younger women chasing me!"

We all laughed as we started back to the ranch.

"It's coming," said Bud. "It's starting right now."

"What's that?" The new hand was curious.

"The Chinook," replied Bud. "Feel it? The wind is already starting to get warmer! It won't take long once it gets going. Before long we're going to have a lot of water."

As we drove back to the ranch, I listened to Bud explain to the new hand what his job would be and what was expected of him. Bud made it clear. I hoped the youngster was listening.

His name was Jimmy McIntyre. He was only sixteen, yet Bud made it clear to him that he was expected to do a man's work and carry his share of the load. Occasionally, Bud would ask, "You got anything to add, Honey?"

I was trying to watch Jimmy's reaction to what Bud was telling him but couldn't see him very well. I thought Bud was doing a good job and I didn't have anything to add. I was more concerned with how this Jimmy McIntyre was taking what Bud was telling him. I got to thinking that what Bud was telling him was pretty basic—people were raised and grew up with the values Bud was outlining. But Bud was being very explicit. I got to thinking that if it was up to me, I'd tell him what to do, let him go do it and either sink or swim on his own. And I wondered why Bud was going to the lengths with this youngster that he was going to. I decided that later when we were alone, I would question Bud about it.

When we arrived at the ranch, supper was ready. It was good to be home, even though I was very limited in what I could do. I hobbled around on crutches and greeted everyone. I had a very tough time picking up Ginny on crutches but managed to do it and sit down. I endured some good-natured kidding from Pat, Dwight, and Chuck about losing some toes, but it was all done in fun. Jimmy was very quiet during supper, but very attentive and listening closely to what was said.

After supper, I questioned Bud about his being so detailed with Jimmy as he explained Jimmy's duties. Bud called Pat, Dwight, and Chuck in to listen after Jimmy went to the bunkhouse to turn in.

"Jimmy comes from more than a broken home," said Bud. "He's adopted and he was adopted at an older age. He was overlooked by many prospective parents because he was a little older and most young prospective parents want to adopt a younger child so they can raise him as their own. He was abandoned at an early age and really doesn't remember or know his real parents. His adoptive parents, my friends John and Mary McIntyre, couldn't have children. They tried for years, so they ended up adopting Jimmy and giving him their name."

"How'd he come to end up here?" Chuck was curious.

"I'm getting to that," replied Bud. "Jimmy has gotten into

a lot of trouble in the past, mostly minor stuff. John and Mary thought if he had a job and could be recognized for his accomplishments, it might help him. They seem to think he's gotten into trouble because he's trying to attract attention to himself. He's been ignored so much in the past he's come to think of himself as a non-person, totally useless. That attitude has given him a very low opinion of himself. We're going to try to straighten him out and get some work out of him at the same time."

"So, we've got to handle him with kid gloves," I said.

"Most certainly not," Bud exclaimed. "He's to be treated just like any other hand! But if you give him a compliment, make sure it's genuine, not just gratuitous. If he needs a chewing out, make sure it's deserved. The kid is just a little mixed up. Perhaps we can help him by giving him some real life lessons out here on the ranch and not in town where there are a lot of people.

"He's a city kid, so he has a lot to learn about a lot of things out here. You fellers need to exercise a little patience with him, but don't be slack in your expectations of him. I'll line him out each day with what to do, you guys just have to make sure he does it. Don't do it for him, but if he needs some help, give it to him.

"When Honey here gets back on his feet, he'll take his orders directly from him."

Pat was strangely quiet during Bud's discourse, but I noticed him nodding his head in agreement as Bud talked.

"Does that mean we have to call Honey Doctor Honey?" I could tell that Dwight was trying to be funny.

"Could we shorten that to Doc?" Chuck was getting into the act.

"I don't know …" Bud said.

"Most assuredly," I interrupted. "Most assuredly!"

"I don't know," continued Bud. "That might not be appropriate. Don't show this youngster any special consideration. I've let him know what's expected of him and he's willing to try. His folks deserve more."

"You mean we're doin' this for his folks an' not so much for him." Pat's comment was more of a statement than a question.

"That's partially right," answered Bud. "We're doing it for all three of them. Now for the good news! A Chinook's coming. Soon they'll be water running all over the place. I can feel it. We won't have much more of this blasted cold weather to deal with. I just hope it dries out before the dudes arrive."

"I'm ready for some warm weather," said Pat. "It's been about ten, maybe fifteen years since we've had a winter like this. It seems like it's gettin' harder for me to take this cold weather."

"I know the feeling," said Bud, "I know the feeling!"

The next morning the water had started running—the warm winds had come. It had warmed up considerably, not enough to walk around in shirt sleeves, but enough to shed one layer of clothing.

Pat, Chuck, and Dwight took Jimmy and started out to do the morning chores. I stood in the doorway of the lodge on my crutches and watched them leave, wondering if Jimmy would do all right. Bud noticed my apparent concern and said, "It's up to him. If he can follow directions, he'll be all right. If not, well, at least he's not in town where he can get into trouble with the other kids his age."

"I wonder if it's a good idea to have him around when the dudes show up," I said.

"Come that time, we'll know what he's going to be. After all, we've got better than a month and a half. And we can give him some special instructions if he's still around when the dudes come."

"Still," I said, "I wonder if it will work out."

"Of course it will," said Bud. "We're only trying to give him an honest shot at life, like most of the rest of us had. He's been ignored for so long he's got a distorted outlook on life. John and Mary tried that by giving him practically everything he wanted. But it seems like he only valued those things he stole or lied to get. We'll give him a real chance to earn what he wants. When he finds out that he doesn't have to lie, cheat, and steal to get what he wants, he'll probably change his outlook on life. I don't think it's all his fault, I'm guessing he's probably a victim of the times. His problem is his reaction to the circumstances."

"When did you acquire your degree in psychology?"

Bud laughed. "I don't have a degree," he said. "But every now and then we get a chance to make a difference. Sometimes it works, sometimes it doesn't, but we have the opportunity to try now. That's the important part, when the opportunity presents itself, we must take advantage of it. Sometimes, just making the effort is rewarding even if the results fall short of the expectations."

I was getting the impression Bud was lecturing me on some pretty important life lessons. It sounded good, but I was really skeptical; I was results-oriented and really wanted the results to turn out as expected. I couldn't see the value in trying something not knowing what the outcome was going to be.

"It's very possible you could have been in the same situation as Jimmy. You were fortunate enough to be born of good parents and raised on a ranch. So was I. A ranch is the best place to raise kids, being around livestock and assuming responsibility for them at a young age is always good for youngsters. It won't hurt Jimmy.

"I've instructed Dwight or Chuck to help Jimmy load hay while Pat and whoever doesn't help Jimmy check the first calvers and the cows. He'll need some constant supervision until he realizes we're depending on him. It might be a good idea to make him believe we're depending on him more than we actually are."

"Are you tryin' to trick that kid into believin' he's somethin' different than what he is?"

Bud laughed again. "No," he said. "We're actually going to trick him into believing he's something worthwhile—valuable as a person and not just a non entity. He's just a little mixed up.

"You better come get inside, you're still recovering. Take it easy. It's warming up, but it isn't really warm yet. It'll take a few says for the Chinook to take effect, if it keeps up."

Sally arrived at my side and closed the door. "You need to take your medicine, Honey." She handed me some pills and another cup of coffee. "These will help fight the infection that's possible with this sort of stuff."

I took the pills and coffee and sat down by the fire. I didn't know what I was going to do to be helpful while I was laid up and I knew I was going to get bored real quick.

When Pat, Chuck, Dwight, and Jimmy showed up for the noon meal, Pat made the comment, "It's warmin' up nicely. I'm figurin' on startin' to halter break the weaner colts in a week or so, if we can get the chores done a little faster. Jimmy was a big help loadin' the hay this mornin'. We'll see how good he is at unloadin' it this afternoon."

Jimmy asked, "You mean we're going to have to unload what I loaded?"

"Yep," answered Pat.

"Then why did I load it?"

Everyone laughed. "When you loaded it, you were actually preparin' a meal for the cattle. When we unload it, we'll be feedin' 'em," answered Pat.

"So, I'm a cattle cook," stated Jimmy.

Again everyone laughed.

"Not exactly," said Bud. "We don't have to cook for the cattle. You're more of a cattle feeder, a cattle caretaker. If we don't take care of them, they won't provide for us."

"It's a two-way street," added Pat. "If we do a good job, those cows will reward us."

"How?" Jimmy was becoming confused.

I could see that Jimmy was becoming lost in the idea of taking care of cattle expecting a reward as the outcome. He hadn't a clue as to how the cattle business worked. He probably thought steaks and hamburger came from the grocery store.

The evening chores were completed early, and Jimmy, Chuck, and Dwight loaded the hay for the next day's feeding. Jimmy was good help loading the hay. Quite often inexperienced help gets in the way doing these chores, but after he was shown what we were doing, he got the hang of it and was a help rather than a hindrance.

The Chinook winds came and the snow started to melt. Soon we had water running everywhere, even where we didn't want it. The wind didn't feel that warm, but it was warm enough to melt the snow.

Slowly but surely I was getting along on my crutches. It was a little difficult, compensating for my missing toes, trying to walk without the crutches. After two weeks and another visit to the doctor, I was given the okay to discontinue using the crutches, although I had been trying to get around without them when Sally or someone else wasn't around. It was a relief to put the crutches away even though I had a slight limp.

Sally noticed the limp and asked, "Is it still hurting you?"

"Not really," I answered

"Then why the limp?"

"I ain't used to walkin' like this. It'll go away soon as I get the hang of walkin' again." I started to put my coat on to go out and help with the chores.

"I hope so," said Sally, smiling. "Your walk looks painful. It might not be good for business with the dudes. With Daddy in the wheelchair, Missus Abercrombie getting older, and you limping, the guests might think this is a rest home for invalids rather than a cattle ranch."

"I've been sayin' that for some time," I said. "Seems like I have to get crippled up before anybody listens to me!"

"Don't say that, Honey. I'm just very concerned about you."

I gave Sally and Ginny a goodbye kiss and started out the door. Ginny was starting to talk, although I couldn't understand her all the time, I did understand a "goodbye" from her.

"You be careful out there," Sally yelled as I started toward the barn. "And don't be tracking mud into the lodge when you come in!"

"Yes ma'am," I answered, tipping my hat. The wind was warmer than when I froze my toes. "I ain't goin' to worry 'bout freezin' my feet!"

I made my way to the barn through the mud and water. The snow was still melting although it was melting fast. The ground had soaked up all the water it could hold and excess water was running off. There was a lot of mud and the going was tough. Watching the runoff, I thought to myself, *The waterholes should be full this year. Leastways, we shouldn't have to go out huntin' the broodmare bunch.*

I made it to the barn where Pat, Dwight, Chuck, and Jimmy were working with the weaner colts and getting them halter broke and broke to lead. Jimmy was having some trouble and Pat was giving him a hand. "Take it easy with him. He's still a baby an' what he learned yesterday he's probably already forgot. Repetition is the key. Do the same thing the same way all the time an' he'll eventually learn. Just go easy with him an' don't expect too much at any one time. He'll come around eventually."

Pat saw me standing inside the barn and started over in my direction. "Just keep workin' him an' don't make any sudden movements. Remember, he's just as scared as you are," said Pat. He was still talking to Jimmy as he approached me.

"The kid's kinda rough on the colts," said Pat, as he sat down

111

on a hay bale next to me. "Kinda reminds me of someone else from my younger days."

I responded, "Really?" I was a little surprised, as Pat hadn't said much about his younger days. I guessed the someone else he was referring to was himself.

"Yep. I think the kid's scared of bein' showed up by Chuck or Dwight or anybody else an' doesn't want that to happen. He's afraid to admit he don't know as much as everyone else. I really think the colts are learnin' faster than him."

"Is there any hope for him?" I was wondering if we were going to be able to keep him around. He was good for the heavy work but I wondered if he could be trusted with the dudes and the finer points of horse handling.

"There's always hope," replied Pat. "I think the feller I'm rememberin' turned out all right." There was a slight smile on Pat's face as he made his last comment and went back to working the colt he had been working with before he stopped to help Jimmy.

I watched everyone working at gentling the colts they had. Pat, of course, was all right, Dwight and Chuck were learning and the lessons they had learned in the past had been well learned. Jimmy was still a question and I decided I'd hold judgment on him until later. I hadn't really had a chance to work with him in person. Wanting to get back to work, I asked, "Which one of these colts needs the most work? I'm ready to get started!"

"The black and white colt on the end has been giving me a lot of trouble," said Dwight.

I started toward the colt Dwight pointed out.

"Watch him," said Dwight. "He's bad to strike and I think he enjoys stepping on my toes!"

"I'm missin' three toes," I said. "He ain't got such a big target if he wants to do that to me!"

I approached the colt cautiously but confidently. I sure didn't want to show any fear to the colt.

The colt struck out at me with his left front foot and missed. I side-stepped the blow. Then the colt immediately started to pull back. I moved as fast as I could to the colt's left shoulder.

"What are you doing?" It was Jimmy. He'd stopped what he was doing to watch. Apparently this colt had already developed a reputation among the hands.

"I'm goin' to show this colt that we don't really mean to do him no harm," I said. "Shortly, he's goin' to get tired of pullin' back an' then he'll jump forward. I'll just stay with him an' keep my hands on him all the time. By the time he gets tired again he might know I ain't goin' to hurt him. Soon he'll learn to trust me. But he won't trust me until I trust him. Watch out, he's gettin' ready to make another move!"

I could feel the colt tensing up again as he continued to pull back. The colt jumped forward releasing the tension on the lead rope and his head. I jumped with him, keeping my hands on his neck and back. The colt relaxed a little when he felt the tension release on his head. I started rubbing him with my hands and could feel him relaxing a little.

"That horse is standing on your foot!" Jimmy was excited.

I looked down. The colt was standing on my boot where my toes should have been.

"You're right! Little colt," I said, "you missed! That's the foot that I'm missin' toes on! You'll have to try harder than that in the future!"

Jimmy had a look of amazement on his face. "You didn't even feel that," he said.

"Nope," I said. "I ain't got no feelin' there 'cause I ain't got no toes there."

"Really?" Jimmy was still amazed.

"Yep. Had 'em took off just for situations like this. It's a lot less painful." I continued rubbing and petting the colt as I talked with Jimmy. The colt hadn't moved his foot off my foot.

"I'll probably have the other foot done next winter," I said. "Hand me a curry comb."

Pat, Chuck, and Dwight were having a hard time keeping their laughter silenced. I was feeding Jimmy a line of bull and he was buying it completely.

Jimmy handed me a curry comb and the colt pulled back again as he approached me. I stayed with the colt when he pulled back.

"He's goin' to jump forward again. Look out."

The colt jumped forward and I stayed with him again. He was quicker to relax this time as I brushed him with the curry comb. This might be a little odd, but it certainly wasn't hurting anything.

"Are you really going to have all your toes cut off?" Jimmy was having some doubts about the honesty of the tale I was telling him.

"Sure am," I said. "An old cowboy told me about this trick a while back. He did it the hard way—he only had one toe cut off at a time. Cost him a bunch of money. I'm goin' to save money an' get it all done at once."

"He did it one at a time?"

"Yep," I said. "Had it done so often, he'd ended up gettin' his foot cut off. His one leg is shorter than the other."

Pat, Dwight, and Chuck were flat out laughing.

"I find that hard to believe," said Jimmy.

"Don't let Honey fill you full of bull," said Pat. "He's kinda known for that around the dudes."

"He does have a warped sense of humor," said Chuck.

"It's my story," I said. "An' I certainly can't embellish it!"

"Any more!" added Dwight.

The Outside of a Horse ...

The mud was heavy all over the ranch. The horses were covered with it and we ended up with it all over us. Brushing the mud off the colts became quite a chore on a daily basis, but it was a big help in gentling the colts and getting them used to being handled by people.

The black and white colt that I had been working with was coming along nicely. The constant handling of him really helped and as I was beginning to trust him more, he started to trust me.

I was able to help with the feeding and this sped things up. We were able to spend more time with the colts and Pat, Dwight, Chuck, and I could spend more time checking the first calvers and the cows. Jimmy watched enviously as we saddled our horses to ride through the cattle.

I had noticed Jimmy watching and on the way back from checking the cattle one morning, I said to Pat, "Why don't we run in the dude horses an' get one for Jimmy? He's showed a lot of interest in ridin' when we've been saddlin' up in the mornin'."

"Has he said anything?"

"No," I answered, "but he's been watchin' pretty close. I think he's probably wishin' he could come along."

"Let's do that," said Pat. "He's been workin' pretty hard with loadin' the hay an' he has been willin' to do about anything. A little horseback ride every day might make a nice reward for him."

We ran the dude horses in and Pat selected a horse for Jimmy. The horse he selected was a dude horse, but the horse needed an experienced rider and didn't get used much.

"We'll let Jimmy put some miles on Digger here. It's about time he started earnin' more of his keep," said Pat, as he roped the horse.

"Don't you think he might be a little too much horse for the kid?"

"No," said Pat. "He'll either learn how to ride or he'll walk. I'll top him off before Jimmy gets on. While I'm toppin' him off, you can explain the neck reinin' to him. I don't think he's ever rode before."

Pat saddled Digger and untracked the horse. I asked Jimmy, "Have you ever rode before?"

"No," was Jimmy's reply.

"Well, you're goin' to learn today," I said and I started explaining how to control the horse. "Get on the fence here." We both climbed onto the top rail of the fence.

"Neck reinin' is how we turn the horse. It's usin' your hands, legs, an' shiftin' your body in the saddle to get the horse to do what you want him to. It's communication between you and the horse, but it's a silent communication. The better you do it, the better your horse will respond. The horse responds to pressure."

As I was explaining this to Jimmy, Pat put a foot in the stirrup and got on Digger. The horse just stood still while Pat got on. When Pat started to turn Digger, the horse took a big jump high in the air and he kicked out with his rear feet. And he continued to buck. Pat rode him without a problem.

"Holy cow!" exclaimed Jimmy, "did Pat tell him to do that?"

I laughed. "No, the horse ain't been rode all winter an' he's just feelin' good. He'll settle down shortly. He's actually a pretty fair horse."

Pat let the horse buck and when he stopped, Pat loped him

around the corral a few times. He stopped him, turned him both directions a few times, and loped him around some more. He rode the horse to where Jimmy and I were sitting on the fence, got off, and handed the reins to Jimmy.

"Your horse is ready for you now," said Pat.

Jimmy scrambled down off the fence and the horse shied away.

"Slow an' easy," said Pat. "Slow an' easy."

It was easy to see that Jimmy was excited about riding the horse. But, after watching the horse buck, he was a little reluctant to get on.

"Go ahead," said Pat, "get on. He should be all right now."

Jimmy was still reluctant.

"Go ahead, Jimmy," I said. "It's sorta like the colts. When you start trustin' us, we can start trustin' you."

Jimmy approached the horse. Pat held Digger's head and instructed Jimmy on how to get on. Jimmy took a tight rein and started to get on.

"Loose rein, loose rein," said Pat, adjusting the slack in Jimmy's reins. "He ain't goin' no wheres, I got him."

Jimmy got on, although it was not as graceful as a seasoned rider. Pat stepped back and let his hold on Digger go. Pat came to the fence where I was sitting and got up on the top rail next to me.

"Another dude," said Pat, as he settled himself on the fence.

"Another dude," I said, as I watched. "Oh well, we've taught a lot of people how to ride over the years. Only this time it's different, we're payin' him. All the others paid us!"

Pat smiled at my comment and turned his attention to Jimmy.

"Just walk the horse in a circle," said Pat, indicating that Jimmy should move the horse. "You don't have to put a quarter in him to get him to move!"

Pat turned to me and said, "You're right, just another dude.

But I'll bet he's a city kid that has had to force his way or fight for whatever he's wanted or got."

"I bet you're right," I said. "It shows in the way he acts around the horses. He's used to gettin' his way by force. He'll have to change, that don't work with the horses an' it generally don't work good with people."

"That's right," replied Pat. "However, this is the perfect place to teach him different. Who was it, Winston Churchill or Will Rogers that said, 'The outside of a horse is good for the inside of a man'? I don't remember."

Pat turned his attention to Jimmy. He was sitting on the horse and neither one of them had moved. "Move him out!"

Jimmy kicked the horse hard and the horse jumped forward.

"Don't kick him," hollered Pat. "Just touch him with your heels. Didn't Honey tell you what to do?"

"Yes," said Jimmy, nervously. "But …"

"Just do what Honey told ya. You know, he's rode more than once. Now turn the horse to the left, usin' your hands an' feet. That's it. Now turn him right. That's it. Give him a loose rein, you're holdin' him too tight. Give him his head an' he'll do what you want him to. That's it. See how good he responds when you don't have constant pressure on the bit in his mouth? Now, you ride him around in the corral an' we'll all go out for a ride."

I knew we were going for a ride for Jimmy's benefit.

"I'll go ahead an' kinda weave my horse around like a drunk an' you an' Jimmy follow. You can point out to the kid what I'm doin' an' maybe he'll get the idea," said Pat.

"You'll need to exaggerate your leg an' heel movements so Jimmy can see 'em. Sometimes your cues to the horse are almost imperceptible. We're givin' the kid a crash course in ridin'," I said. "We generally take longer with the ridin' we teach to the dudes."

"That's right," answered Pat. "But remember, we're payin' him. The dudes are payin' us!"

I laughed. "Seems like I've heard that somewheres before!"

"You may have, you may have! As a matter of fact, I think you said it not too long ago."

"You know, if you're goin' to quote me, you need to give me credit for it."

"I'll give you credit for it, you know your credit is always good with me," said Pat.

"I don't think I'll get rich an' famous with you carryin' my credit," I said.

"Maybe not rich an' maybe not famous, but certainly well known!" Pat laughed at his own joke.

This good-natured bantering continued while Jimmy rode his horse. When it came time for us to go on a longer ride, I told Dwight and Chuck to continue with the halter breaking of the colts. I continued, "We'll need to get that finished up pretty quick so we can start ridin' the comin' two-year-olds. We'll have plenty to do then."

Pat, Jimmy, and I started out.

"Jimmy, you an' me will follow Pat. I don't know where he's goin', but we'll just follow an' find out. We'll do what he's doin' only more of it."

"What for?" Jimmy was curious.

"To be honest with you, this exercise is to teach you how to use your feet and body to communicate with the horse. When Pat goes to the right, we'll go to the right, only farther. Same thing to the left. When we get done you'll have had a crash course in neck reinin'. But don't think you'll know it all when we get done. You'll have to do it enough that it becomes second nature to you an' you'll do it without havin' to think about it."

"How long will that take?"

"Might take the rest of your life, might take only a year or two," I answered. "Depends on you, how hard you work at it."

"I'll certainly try," said Jimmy.

And he did. He watched Pat closely and when Pat used his heels on the horse, Jimmy used his.

"Remember to use your reins," I instructed. "With your reins, you're tellin' the horse what you want him to do. With your heels, you're gettin' him to do it."

A time or two, Jimmy kicked Digger and the horse jumped sideways.

"Easy," I cautioned. "Easy. When you kick him hard, he thinks you want him to move sideways fast. Just take it easy. The horse wants to do what you want him to. You just need to communicate clearly with him. When you see Pat using his heels, try applyin' pressure with the inside of your legs rather than using your heels. The horse will respond. An' it'll make you a better rider."

Jimmy tried it and it worked for him.

That's it. You're gettin' it now. Just keep it up."

We rode for about an hour and a half. When we returned, we unsaddled our horses and turned them loose.

"That's a lot of work to ride a horse," said Jimmy.

"Not really," said Pat. "You're just not used to it. When it becomes second nature an' you don't have to think about what you're doin', it gets a lot easier. How did he do, Honey?"

"He was workin' so hard at doin' what he was supposed to, that I got tired watchin' him! I hope we don't have to do more sessions like this, you guys might wear me out!"

All three of us laughed and it was the first time I had seen Jimmy join wholeheartedly in a laugh.

"Out of deference to you Honey, not wantin' to work you too hard an' wanting to prolong your life, that will be the last ridin' lesson Jimmy gets until he needs another one. It's up to him to regularly use what he's learned. You'll have to work at it, Jimmy. Of course, we can answer questions when necessary."

"I can do that," replied Jimmy enthusiastically. "And I want to thank you guys for taking the time to show me, I really appreciate it!"

Pat looked a little surprised and I suppose I registered some surprise, too. A thank you from Jimmy! When we had tried to help him in the past, our efforts were generally answered with a simple "Yeah."

Not wanting to show my surprise, I said, "Well, let's get back to work. We have a bunch of colts that need gentlin'."

"Yes sir!" Jimmy turned and walked to where Dwight and Chuck were brushing the colts. His walk was different, he walked like he had a purpose, rather than shuffling along like he really didn't want to go.

As Pat and I watched him go, I said, "That's a pleasant surprise!"

"Most assuredly," said Pat, "most assuredly! An' a 'thank you' to boot! I can't hardly believe it."

"An' a 'Yes sir!' That's remarkable," I added.

"This may be a big day for the kid," said Pat. "Even though the 'Yes sir' wasn't called for. Did you see the way he walked to the barn?"

"The 'Yes sir' was warranted," I said, half jokingly. "An' I did see how he walked to the barn. We may have witnessed a drastic change in attitude for the better. An' you did it, Pat."

"Naw," said Pat. "The horse did it."

"The horse did it? Nope," I said. "You did it. Pure an' simple."

"Naw," replied Pat. "The horse did it. Has somethin' to do with 'the outside of a horse is good for the inside of a man.' Who was it that said that?"

Pat and I joined the others in the barn. As we walked to the barn, I told Pat, "We should bring in the yearlin's an' work them a day or two just to refresh their memories then run in the comin' two-year-olds and start ridin' 'em. That cold spell we had put us behind schedule an' we've got dudes comin' before too long. Maybe we should turn the broodmare band out an' let them start grazin' the grass. We could save a lot of feed an' the grass should be comin' with it warmin' up like it has."

"That might work," replied Pat. "But I think we ought to ride over the broodmare range just to see how the grass is comin'."

"Good thinkin'. We'll do that tomorrow an' we can run in the yearlings on the way back. I've got to get ready to start breedin' the heifers. There's a lot to do. Do you want to take Jimmy to gather the yearlings? He ain't rode much an' it could get kinda western."

"We'd best leave him here, for his own safety. We'll kinda put him in charge of the halter breakin' for a few days. That should make him feel like he's got an important job to do, although the colts are comin' along fine an' we could stop any time."

"Well, I'm really pleased with today's results with him. I think there's been a real improvement," I said.

"Yep," said Pat. "The outside of a horse ..."

"Oh shut up! You did a good job!"

"Yes sir," said Pat.

"Oh shut up!"

I knew Pat was kidding with me, as there had never been such formality on the ranch before. But I wanted him to know that he had done a good job with Jimmy. Maybe he only came up with the idea of using the horse to do it, but it brought positive results and it was his idea.

Pat and I rode the broodmare range the next day and decided we would wait a week or ten days before we turned the broodmares out. The grass was coming, but we thought we might give it a little head start.

"The horses will get to goin' after that fresh grass an' lose a lot of weight. There's not enough energy in it to keep 'em in shape an' they'll need all the energy they can get when they start foalin'," said Pat.

"We should have enough feed to keep 'em a week or ten days," I said. "That should suffice."

During the next few days, there was a marked change in Jimmy's attitude. He was left alone to brush and handle the younger colts while the rest of us gathered the yearlings and coming two-year-olds. We managed to take him horseback with us when we checked the cows. We were pretty well done calving out the first calf heifers and I took Jimmy with me one day to check them. I could see he was impressed by the way my horse side-passed opening and closing the gates.

He asked, "How do you get him to do that?"

"Do what?" I was so used to working with my horse, I didn't have to think about what we were doing.

"Move sideways like he did opening the gate."

I had to think before I answered. My horse had opened and closed so many gates that he knew what we were going to do when we moved into position. Often, he would anticipate what we were doing and start to side pass before I was ready. "It's all in the communication between me an' the horse," I said. "Plus the fact that he has done this so much, he knows what we're doin'. The cues I'm givin' him ain't no different than the cues you give your horse when you're turnin' him. All these horses will side pass although some of the dude horses haven't done it for quite a while. It's just a matter of doin' it an' doin' it often."

Jimmy was learning and it seemed like he had a renewed interest in the ranch and his chores. Before he had been quiet and didn't communicate much, now he was opening up and even joking with Dwight and Chuck. He wasn't sure how to take jokes on himself, but Dwight and Chuck didn't cut him any slack.

We started riding the two-year-old colts after a couple of days of brushing and saddling them. Pat or I would snub the colts and Chuck or Dwight would get on them. Then we'd lead them around to get them used to being ridden. Jimmy even wanted to get a colt that he could break and we let him. We had a few of the colts want to buck a little, but by being snubbed close they couldn't do much.

On the better days, Sally and Ginny would come down to the corral to watch and Bud and Missus Abercrombie would ride down in the four-wheeler.

Slowly but surely, we were making progress, although I was becoming increasingly anxious. The spring was passing rapidly and the dudes would be arriving soon. Bud and Sally still had to hire the maids and a cook's helper. Our reservations for the summer were full and if we were to take in any more guests, we'd have to build more cabins. I wasn't sure if we were ready for the dudes, but they would be arriving whether we were ready or not.

In addition to starting the two-year-old colts we still had to bring in the dude horses and ride each one of them just to take off the rough edges. It wasn't hard work, just time consuming and we were running out of time.

A few days later, after we had run in the dude horses and were riding them to take off the rough edges, Sally came down to the corral.

"Daddy wants to talk to you up in the lodge," she said. "It's quite important."

"I'll just walk back with you," I said. "What's this about?"

"I'm not sure," replied Sally.

As we walked to the lodge, I noticed the sheriff's car parked in front of the lodge. I had been busy and hadn't seen him drive in. I walked in the lodge and shook hands with the sheriff. There was another man with him.

"What have I done?" I asked, trying to be funny.

"I don't know what you've done, Honey, you'll have to tell me," answered the sheriff.

"I think Bud an' Sally can tell you I ain't done much around here," I said.

We all laughed at my comment.

"This visit isn't about you, Honey," said the sheriff. "It's about a young feller named Jimmy McIntyre. Do you know him?"

"Yes, he's workin' here. He don't know much but he's learnin'."

"Well," continued the sheriff, "it seems that this Jimmy McIntyre is on probation and he hasn't checked in with his probation officer for some time. This is his probation officer, Mister Mason."

As I shook hands with Mister Mason, he said, "Just call me Bill."

He didn't look like I thought a probation officer should look. He was short, balding, and pudgy. He had a glass eye that constantly looked toward his other eye giving the impression that he was cross-eyed. He didn't project a tough guy image. But he did have the power of the law behind him.

"What has Jimmy done?" I knew the kid was a problem but didn't know he'd been in trouble with the law.

"Mostly just minor stuff," replied Mister Mason. "But there has been enough of it that he's headed for reform school. He's a repeat offender and it appears he's becoming an habitual. The judge that put him on probation told me that he was definitely headed for reform school if he showed up in his court one more time. He also said Jimmy would be there now if it wasn't so crowded. I'm afraid when I take him back, that's where he's going. Unfortunately, most of these repeat offenders eventually end up going to prison."

"Now wait a minute," interrupted Bud. "Is that necessary? He's been out here on the ranch, and hasn't been able to go to town. He certainly hasn't gotten into trouble out here."

"But he hasn't contacted me for two months and he's supposed to check in with me twice a month. He's broken the terms of his probation. I'm afraid I'll have to take him back with me."

"That seems kinda harsh to me," I said. "Facin' time in reform school for failin' to say hello a couple of times a month. An' just when he was comin' along so good."

Bud had a surprised look on his face.

"Yes," said Bud, as he quickly regained his composure. "The youngster has been working out well here. He's got chores and responsibilities that he's responding to and accepting exceptionally well."

"Failing to check in with his probation officer on time does not indicate an acceptance of responsibility," said Mister Mason.

"But we've had him awful busy here," I said. I couldn't believe I was sticking up for the kid, but I was. I was actually enjoying watching him change and his change was positive. "Bud hired him while I was in the hospital havin' part of my foot amputated 'cause I couldn't do much then. He helped out with the everyday chores an' made things easier for the other hands. He's been involved in virtually every aspect of what we're doin' here, from feedin' to breakin' colts. He gets along good with the other hands an' does his work without complainin'."

"He gets along with the other hands?" Mister Mason suddenly showed more interest. "He's always been a loner, he never was in a gang or anything like that."

"Yep," I replied. "An' the other hands like him. I'm real pleased with his work. An' it has been interestin' watchin' his improvement."

"It sounds to me like you've got some free labor here and you don't want to lose it," said Mister Mason. He was listening closely and not missing anything.

Bud became a little agitated. "That's not the case! He's being paid a wage equal to his abilities and skills. He's not making as much as my other hands because he hasn't got the experience, but I'm willing to increase his pay as he gets better."

Mister Mason appeared to ignore Bud and asked me, "What do you mean by improvement?"

"By improvement I mean that when he came here he had a poor attitude. A poor outlook. He did what he was told, but almost grudgingly. He almost acted like he was a prisoner. We had him helpin' us halter break some colts an' he acted like everything he'd ever accomplished was accomplished through the use of force. We got him to slow down or ease up on the colts an' he could see some results.

"Then we got him horseback and taught him to ride and communicate gently with his horse. That's when we noticed the big change. When he saw we got results doin' what we were doin' an' he got results by doin' the same thing, his whole attitude changed. He began walkin' with a little spring in his step an' even began smilin' some. I think he even looks forward to goin' to work every day. We've given him some chores to do on his own an' he hustles through those chores so as he can work with the horses. Now he's got a chance to ride every day and improve his newly acquired skills. He acts like he's got a purpose in life. Why he even surprised us by thankin' us the other day! In my opinion, he's on his way to a complete turn around."

"A complete turn around is three hundred and sixty degrees. He'll end up where he started," said Mister Mason.

"By a complete turn around, I mean a hundred and eighty degrees. Once he gets turned around proper, he won't want to turn back."

Mister Mason was contemplating something. I didn't know what, but he seemed perplexed. He said, "I'd like to talk to Jimmy."

"I'll go down to the corral an' get him," I volunteered.

"I'll go with you," said Mister Mason.

"It's plenty muddy out there," I said.

"That's all right, I'll go with you. I insist."

"There's some extra overshoes on the porch," said Bud. "I'll get them for you."

Bud started wheeling himself toward the porch.

Mister Mason sat down and put on the overshoes Bud gave him.

"I can get him," I volunteered again as I started out the door. "Do you want to go sheriff?"

"No," said Mister Mason, "I'll go with you. I don't need you prompting Mister McIntyre about what he's doing here."

The sheriff indicated that he would remain in the lodge and visit with Bud.

We started toward the corrals and I said, "You're not very trustin' are you." It was a statement rather than a question.

"In my line of work, a person has to be very skeptical. It's become a source of annoyance to my wife," replied Mister Mason.

"You mean you don't trust your wife?"

"No! But sometimes that's what she thinks!"

I smiled at Mister Mason's reply. We reached the corrals and I said, "Jimmy, come over here. You have a visitor."

Jimmy turned and as soon as he saw Mister Mason his demeanor changed. The smile on his face faded. He was riding a colt and Pat had the colt snubbed up. Slowly he stopped what he was doing as Pat led the colt to where Mister Mason and I were climbing on the fence.

"You haven't contacted me, Mister McIntyre," said Mister Mason. "You're in violation of the terms of your probation. What do you have to say for yourself?"

"Nothing," said Jimmy as he shrugged his shoulders, "Except that I forgot and they've kept me pretty busy here."

"Didn't you think to even call?"

"No sir," answered Jimmy.

"Don't you get a day off to come to town and check in?"

"No sir," replied Jimmy. "But nobody else gets a day off and I really don't want to go to town. I get bored in town."

"Where did you learn to ride?"

"Right here," said Jimmy. His demeanor changed a little and I could tell he felt a little better. "They taught me how. There's more to this than just sitting here."

"How come he's leading you around?"

"This is a young horse and we're teaching him how to be ridden."

"Isn't that like the blind leading the blind?"

"Not exactly, Mister Mason. You see, I already know a little more than this horse," replied Jimmy.

Mister Mason looked surprised. I was even a little amazed at Jimmy's answer.

"You've put me in a difficult position," said Mister Mason. "You go about your business while I contemplate this."

I motioned to Pat to lead them away and they left with Mister Mason watching closely. Shortly we started back toward the lodge.

"There has been a definite change in the boy," he said. "It appears to be a change for the better. How did you do it?"

"I'm not sure," I said. "But Pat is always sayin' 'the outside of a horse is good for the inside of a man.' That might have something to do with it."

"Ah," said Mister Mason. "Winston Churchill!"

"Or Will Rogers."

"Yes. Who did say that? Now, about the situation at hand. As I see it, we have two alternatives. I can take Mister McIntyre back with me, put him in juvenile detention until the judge can decide whether or not to send him to reform school. That was my original intention and why I had the sheriff bring me out here. I really don't like that option in light of the change I've seen in the boy in the very short time we visited.

"Or I can leave him here, under your direct supervision until his probation period is up. Then he'll be free to go anywhere he wants to."

"Hold on here, Bill," I said, "I don't want your job! I'm gettin' along pretty good with my wife!"

Mister Mason laughed. "You wouldn't be getting my job although you would need to report to me regularly with regard to Mister McIntyre. And he would still need to contact me every two weeks."

"In person? I don't know that I can get myself or Jimmy into town all that often."

"A phone call would suffice. What do you think of the idea? I really hate putting these young people in the detention system—it doesn't seem to help them much in the long run. Our success rate in detention is not very good. And I think I could get the judge to go for the idea."

"You mean prison, don't you?"

Mister Mason shrugged his shoulders. "I guess so. It's a very depressing part of my job. What do you think?"

"I'm not sure. Let's talk it over with Bud an' see what he thinks. Now, about that problem with your wife, why don't you let us take you for a horseback ride? You know, the outside of a horse is good for the inside of a man!"

Mister Mason was laughing as we entered the lodge. The sheriff and Bud were still visiting as we entered.

Bud asked, "Well, what did you find out?"

Mister Mason indicated that he had noted a positive change in Jimmy and outlined his plan. Bud showed immediate interest and when the plan was explained, Bud immediately said, "Of course Honey will do it! He'll be glad to! Won't you, Honey!"

"Only with your help," I said. "Of course you realize that we'll be on probation, too!" Everyone laughed.

"Then the matter is settled pending on how the judge feels

about it. I'll send you a written description of what your duties and responsibilities are. You'll have to explain to Mister McIntyre our agreement. If he's not in agreement with it, it's off. Sheriff, we're done here, we can leave any time. Honey, I might take you up on your offer."

"Anytime, Bill, anytime. You'll have a chance to check up on Jimmy an' see how he's doin' on his probation an' you can check up on us an' see how we're doin' on our probation. But remember, if you go ridin' with us, I get to pick the horse you ride!"

Bill laughed. "I don't know if I want one of my 'clients' picking the horse I ride!"

The sheriff and Mister Mason left. I started to go to the corrals, but Bud and Sally stopped me. Bud asked, "What went on down there?"

I told them what had transpired. When I told them about Jimmy sayin' that 'we're trainin' this horse' an' his comment that he knew 'a little more than the horse', Bud clapped his hands together.

"You've made some real progress with that boy, Honey. Good job! I knew you could do it. Sally, can you get a cabin ready? I want Jimmy's folks to come out here and visit their boy. Honey, what changed your mind? I got the impression you didn't much care for the boy."

"I really didn't in the beginning," I said. "But I began to notice a change in the boy and I thought there was something there worth workin' for."

"But you never said anything," said Bud.

"I didn't say anythin' because I wasn't sure. I'm still withholdin' a final judgment. We'll have to see how it turns out."

"That's fair enough," said Bud. "I'll sign the court papers when they come. You won't have to be responsible for that."

A Misfit Crew

We were about done calving out the first calvers. I turned the Black Angus bull in with the heifers that hadn't calved and we started moving the heifers and cows that had calved onto their respective pastures. The grass was coming good and we'd moved the broodmare band out on their range. We were making good progress riding the two-year-old colts and were taking some of them out of the corral on rides. Because of the weather, we'd canceled our spring horse sale.

"We'll just have more horses to sell next year," said Bud. "And we'll have more time to ride the young horses. They'll be better and they'll sell better."

Jimmy's folks came for a visit and, according to Bud, they were impressed with Jimmy and his attitude. He actually greeted them and there seemed to be some real affection on his part towards them. Bud told me later that Jimmy's dad told him, "Jimmy really acts like he's glad to see us rather than just tolerating us as he has done in the past." Bud also said that his dad had volunteered to pay Jimmy's wages but Bud declined to accept any money. Bud told him, "Jimmy has worked hard and earned every cent he has coming to him. I'm glad to pay him."

Jimmy's folks spent three days with us watching Jimmy work. There seemed to be a bond developing between them that hadn't been there in the past. When they left, they asked Jimmy if there was anything they could send him from town. I was surprised by his answer. "I could use some new clothes—pants, shirts, underwear, socks. I also need some boots and a hat. I'll ask Mister Wilson for some money and you can send them out."

The last part of his answer is what surprised me. He actually volunteered to buy his own clothes.

Bud heard his answer and said, "Sally, get the checkbook."

Bud wrote Jimmy a check and Jimmy was surprised at how much it was. "This is too much," he said.

"No," said Bud. "That pays you up to today. But you still have to work the rest of the day and tomorrow." Bud turned toward Jimmy's parents. "Don't worry about the boots and hat, we'll take him to town and get that stuff so he can get it fitted right."

Jimmy showed a sign of relief. For a brief instant he thought he was being paid off and leaving.

Every other Monday morning at 9:00, I had Jimmy come to the lodge and we called Mister Mason. He had convinced the judge that our plan was workable and in Jimmy's best interest. Jimmy was a little disgruntled at having to call every two weeks, but I told him it was necessary. "It's part of our agreement and we have to live up to it." He resigned himself to it and I began to feel like he resented it because it kept him from his chores and cut down his riding time. But his telephone visits with Mister Mason were cordial.

I would generally let Jimmy talk to Mister Mason first. When he was finished, I'd let him go back to work and have a prolonged talk about Jimmy, what he was doing and his progress, with Mister Mason. On occasion, Mister Mason would vent his frustration about other matters to me. He even tried to convince me to take on other parolees.

"We can't do that," I said. "We have other chores to do and our guests are coming. We'll have our hands full shortly. Besides, Bud only volunteered to take Jimmy because he knows Jimmy's folks. What we've done is more like a personal favor. We don't want to become a rehabilitation center for juvenile delinquents. That might be a project you could get some other folks interested in."

I almost felt sorry for Mister Mason. In our biweekly telephone visits, I had come to know the man and come to like him. I always smiled as I pictured him on the other end of the line with his crossed eyes. He just had an unpleasant job. At the end of our conversations, I always invited him out to go for a horseback ride, for his welfare.

He would always say, "We'll see, we'll see."

Bud and Sally took Ginny and went to the college to interview the college kids for the maids' jobs. I found that I missed them, particularly Ginny climbing up on my lap after supper. I would tell her stories that I made up. Often, I would fall asleep before she did and only wake up when I felt Sally taking Ginny to put her to bed. These times after supper were the only times I really had to spend with her. I got to thinking that I needed to spend more time with her or we might end up having a relationship like Jimmy had with his parents. I got to discussing this with Sally one night and she tried to put my fears at ease.

"You're a good daddy," she said. "Ginny's luckier than most kids, she gets to spend time with you occasionally during the day, particularly at the noon meal. Most kids only see their dad in the evening after work. And she's always talking about how she's going to help you with the horses when she gets bigger. And she'll get that opportunity."

"Well," I said, "we've got dudes comin'. We'll have to see if we can improve the situation when we're not so busy."

Sally and Missus Abercrombie had started cleaning a few cabins for some early arrivals. Ginny was supposedly helping. Everyone was busy. In addition to riding the two-year-old colts, we were riding the dude horses.

Before the first guests showed up, I took an inventory of our hired help situation. We had Bud, an invalid confined to a wheelchair or the four-wheeler. Missus Abercrombie, an old woman who couldn't do much but nevertheless tried. My sister Betty, a teenage girl. She was coming to watch Ginny again during the summer. Jimmy, a juvenile delinquent jailbird, and me, a partial cripple. I still walked with a slight limp. At this point in time, the only healthy people on the crew were Sally, Pat, Dwight, Chuck, and the cook.

I was discussing this with Bud one night and made a comment about having a misfit crew.

"That's all right," said Bud. "We'll do just fine! We're ready for the summer!"

Despite his being confined to a wheelchair, I never ceased to be amazed at Bud's positive outlook.

Other Books by Stu Campbell

Horsing Around a Lot

Horsing Around the Dudes

Humor Around Horses

You Can't Be Serious!

Comedy Around the Corral

More Humor Around Horses

A Young Cowboy's Adventure

Honey

Surprise!

Intruders

Expectations